Life On A Tin Can:

The Pacific War

Richard C. Epps

AmErica House
Baltimore

First printing

ISBN: 1-59129-049-X
PUBLISHED BY AMERICA HOUSE BOOK PUBLISHERS
www.publishamerica.com
Baltimore

Printed in the United States of America

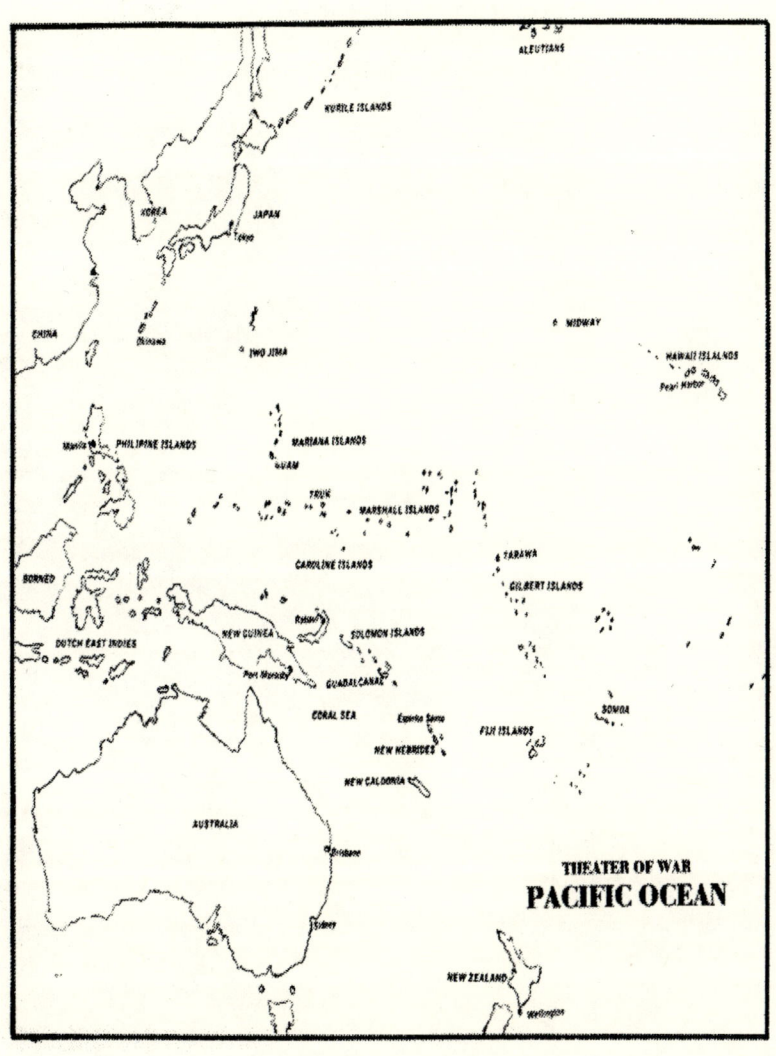

ALEUTIANS

KURILE ISLANDS

KOREA

JAPAN

Tokyo

CHINA

Okinawa

MIDWAY

IWO JIMA

HAWAII ISLANDS

Pearl Harbor

Manila PHILIPPINE ISLANDS

MARIANA ISLANDS

GUAM

TRUK

MARSHALL ISLANDS

CAROLINE ISLANDS

TARAWA

GILBERT ISLANDS

BORNEO

DUTCH EAST INDIES

NEW GUINEA

Rabaul

SOLOMON ISLANDS

Port Moresby

GUADALCANAL

CORAL SEA

Espiritu Santo

NEW HEBRIDES

FIJI ISLANDS

SAMOA

NEW CALEDONIA

AUSTRALIA

Brisbane

THEATER OF WAR

PACIFIC OCEAN

Sydney

NEW ZEALAND

Wellington

To all of the Tin Can Sailors of World War II,
a job well done

ACKNOWLEDGMENTS

Writing is not one of my strong talents, and this project took me some time to complete. My son James A. Epps, who was a gifted writer, made some helpful suggestions at the start. I am also indebted to my sons-in-law, Mark Woy, Marvin Barker, and to my wonderful wife Jimmie for their patience and tireless labors in proofreading my dull ramblings. My thanks goes out to Professor Janice Albert, and her class on *Writing Memoirs* for their many helpful contributions. I also want to thank Ronald Gunn, and John and Mary Gordon for the helpful suggestions in handling graphics.

All pictures from the U.S. Navy Department -Naval Historical Center are allowed by the following permission: "It's a source of images that are BELIEVED to be in the Public Domain. They can be used by anyone, for any purpose, without obtaining our permission and without payment of usage fees to the Naval Historical Center."

All pictures from the U. S. Naval Institute were printed with permission from the Institute.

All remaining pictures and maps are from my personal files.

CONTENTS

Give me a fast ship with stout men
For I intend to go in harm's way

— John Paul Jones

PREFACE

This paper was originally written to give my children some idea of my activities during the period of 1940 through 1945 in World War II. It covers the highlights of my experiences during that period of the war.

After I was separated from active duty with the U.S. Navy in December 1945, we had one son and my wife was pregnant with our first daughter. I also had to get a job and enroll at the University of California in Berkeley to continue my college education. Needless to say, living conditions got so busy that there was no time to relate any of my WWII experiences to anyone.

As time went on, with increasing activities with family life and working full time, there was little opportunity to convey to anyone my WWII service and the significant events involved.

Today, some of my children are still too busy to sit and listen to the stories of what I did and how I felt during my time of active duty in the U.S. Navy. So I am writing down (to the best of my memory) a chronological record of life aboard a destroyer for anyone who is interested to peruse when they have the time.

There has been reluctance on my part to dwell on going into this subject because I never was involved in any activity that could be construed as an act of bravery. My active duty time was aboard two destroyers that did not receive any major battle damage, and I suffered no wounds during my four and half years of active duty during World War II. This is not to say that my experiences were not exciting, for they were. I experienced more excitement on a continuing basis than I had ever had before, and I had the opportunity to witness some of the largest naval battles of all time. To have been a part of such huge naval operations was truly inspiring, and I was fortunate to have been involved and lucky to have survived.

It was my good luck to have been assigned to a destroyer which served with most of the fast carrier task forces, and to have had a front row seat for a majority of the major combat operations in the Pacific during World War II.

A recent book titled *CROSSING THE LINE: A Bluejacket's World War II Odyssey*, by Alvin Kernan, was most interesting to me in how he related his war experiences. The author had many responses after the first printing in which readers wanted to know how he remembered so many details of his service on two aircraft carriers during the war. His response was that as he sat at the keyboard of his word processor, entering material about certain events, many of his past experiences came to mind. The same phenomenon occurred in my case, as hidden events were uncovered as the writing proceeded. Professor Kernan holds a Ph.D. in English Literature from Yale University and was a professor in English Literature at Yale and Princeton Universities until he retired. His book was so engrossing, that it inspired me to put down some of my experiences during the war.

During my first tour of duty on a destroyer, I kept a diary in a small green notebook. Unfortunately that book was lost after I returned home at the end of the war. Therefore, the events that were experienced will have to come mostly from memory.

The reader may wonder how so many details can be remembered after more than fifty years of elapsed time. It amazed me how so many things kept popping up in my memory as I was describing one experience, another event would come to mind, so I would jot down notes on a pad to be sure to include them in the proper place.

Some of the events experienced during the war are so deeply imprinted on my mind that they remain fresh and vivid today, and will never be lost from my memory bank. I was able to obtain a copies of the ship's deck logs that has been helpful in keeping the chronology of the writing in order.

For those of you who are wondering what "Tin Cans" are, in the U. S. Navy they are what sailors have called our destroyers because these ships had no armor plating. Destroyers have also been referred to as "Greyhounds" because of their high-speed capabilities. John Paul Jones would certainly have enjoyed serving on our World War II destroyers.

As John Steinbeck says, " A destroyer is a lovely ship, probably the nicest fighting ship of all. Battleships are a little like steel cities or great factories of destruction. Aircraft carriers are floating flying fields. Even cruisers are big pieces of machinery, but a destroyer is all boat. In the beautiful clean lines of her, in her speed and roughness, in curious gallantry, she is completely a ship, in the old sense."

Destroyers were the most utilitarian ships in the U.S. Navy during the war. They served in the fast carrier task forces as antisubmarine patrol, they provided needed anti-aircraft fire support, they served as plane guard for the carriers during air operations, and they delivered mail and transferred personnel between the larger ships.

With the advent of radar, some of them also became radar picket ships that would be stationed several miles from the task force in the direction of the enemy target. Here they provided early warning of enemy air attacks, and they provided a checkpoint for our aircraft enroute to their target. They also served as a visual check for our planes returning to the task force to insure that no enemy planes were shadowing our returning aircraft.

To aid in your understanding of Navy terms, there is a glossary at the rear of this book.

1

Pre-December 7, 1941

Motto over the entrance door at Boswell Junior High,
Topeka, Kansas:

**Enter To Learn
Go Forth To Serve**

And did we ever serve

I was born and raised in Topeka, Kansas where I lived in a two-story house with my family. By the time I was ten years old, the great depression had started and money was in very short supply.

The Epps House in Topeka

My parents did not have any interest in radio programs so they did not have a radio in the house. At the time my older brother George was living in the house and he brought a radio home and set it up in the living room for us all to enjoy. I became interested in several programs and when George got married a few years later and moved from the house, he took the radio with him.

I could not afford to buy a new radio so George showed me how to build a crystal set. I enjoyed the crystal set very much, but it could only get the one station in Topeka and I wanted to receive stations in Kansas City and Lawrence. George helped me by getting enough parts to construct a battery radio. By this time, I was in junior high school (grades 7-9) and my interest in short wave developed. With the help of an amateur radio operator, I constructed my first short wave receiver. After listening to some of the amateur radio bands I decided to get an amateur radio license.

With one of my schoolmates, Dave Ballard, we practiced Morse code and studied radio theory. A few months later we went to Kansas City where we took and passed the examination for our amateur radio licenses. During my high school years my favorite activity (outside of football and girls) was operating my amateur radio station.

Upon completing high school the normal course of action was to enroll in the engineering school at the University of Kansas (KU) in Lawrence, Kansas where the other members of the Epps family had graduated. KU was a land grant school and at that time, male students were required to take ROTC training. I did not look forward to being in the U.S. Army so I joined the U.S. Naval Communication Reserve. Since I had an amateur radio license, my enlistment rating should have been Radioman 3rd Class; however, when the papers came through my rate was Apprentice Seaman.

I was already enrolled in my freshman year at KU, and was busy in classes and studying, so I did nothing about getting the rate that had been promised.

In May 1941, while attending my second semester, orders were received for active duty at the U.S. Naval Radio School at Indianapolis, Indiana. I dropped out of school at KU, packed my bag and boarded the train for Indianapolis. The school was located in the Naval Reserve Armory in the city and it was a large concrete building. In the center of the building was a large room, which had been used as a drill floor.

This was where two levels of bunks had been set up to house

recruits. This large area was surrounded by classrooms and a mess hall.

One of the larger rooms had radio operating positions. These positions all had typewriters, headphones for learning to take Morse code on the typewriter, and a telegraph key to the right of the typewriter. Since I am left handed, I started looking around the room for a left handed position. A Chief Radioman asked me what I was looking for and when I told him he informed me, "You are in the Navy now, you're right handed." With practice, I did learn to send on the telegraph key with my right hand.

We had a Boatswain Mate First Class in charge of us outside of classroom instruction. One night there was some noise after lights out and the boatswain mate told us to quiet down. One of the recruits spoke back to him. Nobody would confess, so he took us outside to the drill field and made us run laps for a couple of hours.

In addition to radio classes, we had to go through regular basic training that recruits experienced at recruit training centers.

While cleaning large garbage cans one Saturday, one of the recruits asked a person in khakis, "Hey Chief, where do we put the clean cans?" With that he was about ready to explode, took off his hat and pointed to the gold braid and said, "You dumb bastard, this tells you that I am a commissioned officer and should be addressed as SIR."

In addition to cleanup details like this we did time serving food, cleaning up the building, hand washing and drying our clothes and learning close order drills. We drilled each day and for most of each Saturday. During June and July it was hot and some of the fellows would pass out each Saturday during drills. On Saturday evenings and Sundays, we had liberty and were allowed to leave the armory. One Saturday night, several of us went to a bar and I got my first taste of wine. I didn't like it much and was glad to get out of there as I was taking a ribbing from some of the other fellows.

On Sundays, Walt Feeby and I would go to a grocery store and each get a pie and a quart of milk and sit on a bench in a park and have our fill.

One weekend I made a train trip to Chicago where my sister Katharine was living. She took me to a nightclub where we had dinner and listened to Benny Goodman's orchestra. We had a great time and it sure was good to hear the Goodman band live, after hearing it so many times on the radio.

Even though we were restricted to the armory five days a week, the three months in Indiana were interesting and we learned a lot about the Navy and how to get along.

At the end of the radio school, those of us who had radio licenses were given the choice of going to aviation radio training, or to a school in radar. I was tempted to take aviation radio training because flying in combat aircraft would certainly be an exciting experience and would give one a great view of all of the action, and in the Navy some enlisted men were picked for pilot training. However, since none of us knew what radar was, I decided to go along with the others in choosing the radar training.

This school was conducted at the Naval Research Laboratories just outside of Washington, D.C. We soon found that radar stood for Radio Detection And Ranging. This phenomenon was discovered at the Naval Research Laboratories and in England while communicating at very high frequency (vhf). At both locations they noticed that aircraft flying nearby interfered with the radio signals.

To aid in detecting aircraft the scientists designed the vhf radio transmitter to only send out a short pulse of energy and then they had a receiver at the same location to detect reflected energy from aircraft.

This was the Navy's first radar school and we were fascinated by this new system to detect aircraft and ships. These systems were classified secret and we had to get out of our uniforms and wear civilian clothes to class.

We were given large green notebooks and we kept copious notes while in classes, only to have them collected and burned at the end of the school term.

The instructors told us that taking detailed notes was the best way of remembering, even if we no longer had our notebooks for reference. The air search radar sets that we first studied, were very crude compared to those that we received in the fleet in 1942. Most of the radar transmitting parts came from old high powered radio transmitters. We did have the first fire-control radar to study. This system was designed to give us very accurate bearings and range to targets detected by the search radar.

The beauty of radar ranges was that they were accurate from minimum range to the maximum range of the equipment. If the unit had an error of 10 yards at a range of 200 yards, then it would only be off by 10 yards at 30,000 or 50,000 yards range to the target.

This accuracy of radar ranging was a big improvement over the optical range finder in the main battery gun director. The optical range finder was very accurate at short ranges, but its error increased with each additional yard to the target.

After completing this radar course, we were all excited about the possible application of this new phenomenon to the fleet.

In addition to the three months of class at the Naval Research Laboratories, we had weekends off, giving us an opportunity to see many of the sights around Washington D.C. We went to the Capital Building, the Lincoln and Washington Monuments and the Smithsonian. The visit to the Smithsonian was most fortunate because one of the areas we visited displayed the effects of venereal diseases. The display showing the stages of syphilis was frightening with the final stage display showing the deterioration of the brain. This was enough to keep me later on from going with some of my shipmates to the "cat" houses.

After completing the radar school we were given a month of leave and ordered to report to the Naval Receiving Station in San Diego on November 20, 1941 for transport to Pearl Harbor, Hawaii, to join the Pacific Fleet. I rode the train home to Topeka to see my family and some friends. I really enjoyed my leave as it gave me a chance to strut around town in my uniform. After my leave was up, I said goodbye to my family and boarded another train for San Diego,

California.

Upon arrival at the receiving station, we were assigned bunks in a large barracks room. Since I had arrived alone, I didn't know anybody at the receiving station. At this early stage of my active duty in the U.S. Navy there were very few Naval Reservists on duty so most of the men in the barracks were regular Navy.

One afternoon, after finishing a shower, I returned to my bunk to find my wallet was missing. Apprentice Seaman made only twenty-two dollars a month, therefore, I didn't have anything to fall back on. I put a notice on the bulletin board and within a half an hour the wallet was returned. Another sailor found it in the wash room. Most of the regular Navy sailors were honest and friendly.

At San Diego I ran into Dave Ballard from Topeka, Kansas. The first night we went out with two of his shipmates from the *U.S.S. Lexington* CV-2 to a bar where four of us had our picture taken and had some drinks (not as bad this time).

Later, we went to another bar and as soon as we stepped in the door we saw a riot going on between some marines and sailors. It was just like the movies with guys getting knocked down and with chairs flying around. We decided to get out while the getting was good. This was before we got into the war so the marines had to fight somebody.

Downtown at the U.S. Grant Hotel there was a telephone exchange with an operator on duty. We could give her our desired number, pay, and then she would direct us to the next available phone booth. While waiting for my call to Topeka, I saw a couple of sailors come by with a sack. About half way across the room, one of the fellows dropped the sack and it broke the whiskey bottle inside. Both of them started to cry and take off their white hats and soak up the whiskey and squeeze it into their mouths. I thought it was one of the funniest things I had seen. I had always heard that sailors did some unusual things, and this evening was a good example.

On December 6, 1941 orders were received transferring a group of us to a troop transport bound for Pearl Harbor. Since the ship was not scheduled to leave San Diego until Monday, December 8, 1941 we were granted weekend liberty.

I took a trip on the train to Los Angeles to visit George Chrisman, a high school football buddy, who was living there. We met, had dinner and then we went to the Palladium to hear Stan Kenton's big band. We had a great time as we both loved big band music. We didn't do any dancing or drinking, just enjoyed the music.

We returned to his apartment for the night and early Sunday morning we decided to go to the amusement park in Santa Monica for a roller coaster ride. Just we as walked in the main gate we heard a radio reporting the attack on Pearl Harbor, and ordering all servicemen back to their stations. George drove me to the train station for the return trip to San Diego. At this time I was only 19 and needless to say I was really scared having never been to sea before. Would the Japanese attack the U. S. Naval base at San Diego? Were they going to attack San Francisco? Would they attack the transport we were scheduled to sail on?

It suddenly dawned on me that we would soon be sailing for the point where the United States had suffered an aggressive surprise assault and the ship we would be on was a transport and not a fighting ship. I had been raised in a good neighborhood in Topeka, Kansas where there were six other boys about my age. When we were about six or seven years old, we used to play war in a vacant lot where a house had been torn down. We used the basement walls as trenches and we thought it would be great to be in a real war. Now, thirteen years later, I certainly did not have those same thoughts.

On the train trip back to San Diego, I was beginning to get really scared. Here I was going out into the war area and I felt all alone since I was not with anyone that I knew. What did I get myself into by volunteering for the Naval Reserve so that I wouldn't have to drill in the ROTC at KU?

2

Pearl Harbor

Pearl Harbor

Upon our return to the Naval Station in San Diego on December 7th, we were fed and told to go pack our sea bags and standby for orders to ship out. We were then loaded aboard a troop ship for transport to the Pacific Fleet at Pearl Harbor, Hawaii.

Having never been to sea before, this was a completely new experience for me. We soon got underway on December 8th, 1941, cleared the San Diego harbor and soon the rolling and pitching were upon us. This didn't get to me at first, but the very next morning a boatswain mate 3rd class was put in charge of us, and he picked me to serve in the garbage locker next to the galley. In the garbage locker there was a grinding machine that disposed of all the ship's garbage. After operating the machine for about two hours, the smell got the best of me.

With the movement of the ship I became seasick. Fortunately there was an understanding cook working the galley, and he took me to the bread locker and gave me hardtack, which was like large soda crackers. He told me to eat the hardtack, and when finished with my detail to go topside and look at the horizon. This cured my seasickness and I was never bothered again, even on the rough riding destroyers. Working in the garbage locker most of the time did not give me the opportunity to make many friends. I swore that if I ever saw that third class boatswains mate again, I would get even with him. I did see him again in 1945 on the trip back from Tokyo Bay to San Diego. At that time I was an Ensign, and he was a Chief Boatswain.

I was now four years older and didn't see any reason to bring it up with him.

When not working in the galley area, I loved to go topside and look out at the ocean and feel the roll and pitch of the ship.

27

In the evening it was quite a sight to see the sun set with clouds scattered across the horizon. First, it was yellow, next orange and finally dark red.

Every day, every hour, every minute while awake, we wondered if we would be attacked by a submarine, or maybe a Japanese task force. We were scared, but we kept our fingers crossed and hoped for the best. A thought kept coming to mind; "What am I doing out here while all of my school buddies are safe at home?" Why did I think I was so smart by joining the Naval Reserve instead of the ROTC? About half way to Hawaii, the water smoothed out quite a bit and the ship was riding much better. We finally sighted the Hawaiian Islands and they made a beautiful picture with the tropical mountains offset by the deep blue of the ocean and the light blue of the sky. We swung around the south side of Oahu, and headed for the entrance to Pearl Harbor. As we steamed into the harbor the extent of the damage was so appalling that some of the senior petty officers and chiefs were crying at the horrible sight of their old favorite ships sunk and or damaged.

The bombs and torpedoes ruptured the fuel tanks on all of the larger ships, and the whole harbor was covered with black oil. Looking around the bay, my heart was in my stomach and I couldn't believe my eyes. Most of the damage to ships was concentrated on the battleships and cruisers. The destroyers and other ships that were not damaged were operational. In all there were eighteen United States Naval vessels either sunk or badly damaged at Pearl Harbor on December 7, 1941.

There were four battleships sunk and four badly damaged, and we suffered the loss of 164 Navy and Army aircraft. The United States suffered the loss of 2,403 killed, and 1,178 wounded. Most of the losses were from the Navy.

All the Pacific Fleet aircraft carriers were at sea on December 7th, delivering Marine fighter planes to Wake Island and Midway Island.

After arrival at Pearl Harbor on December 13, 1941, I was transferred to the *U.S.S. Whitney* destroyer tender for further transfer to the Destroyer, *U.S.S. Aylwin, DD355*, that was not in the harbor at that time. My assignment while on the *Whitney* was working with the Chief Sonarman checking out the sonar submarine search systems on the destroyers that were in the harbor. This gave me a chance to learn how the sonar systems operated, and how to repair them.

This was a quick school that lasted about a month and a half, until the *Aylwin* returned to port. While riding the boat from the *Whitney* to the various destroyers we had a chance to look around at the damage to the various ships. The battleships were tied up at their berths at Ford Island. Most of them were salvageable with the exception of the *Arizona*, which had suffered a massive explosion of one of its main ammunition magazines, and the *Oklahoma*, that was capsized. In one of the dry docks, a cruiser and two destroyers were sitting up on blocks. A bomb had exploded next to one of the destroyers knocking it off of the blocks and it was lying on its side.

The battleship *Nevada* had gotten underway during the attack but was hit as it tried to leave the harbor, so the skipper grounded the ship to keep it from blocking the channel. Every day as I looked around while going from ship to ship, I couldn't help but wonder how we had been caught so much by surprise, especially since some of the larger ships already had radar installed.

We worked on the destroyer sonar systems six days a week, and on Sundays we were granted liberty. I went into Honolulu each weekend to look around and to swim in the ocean.

While swimming at Waikiki Beach, a gentleman at the Outrigger Canoe Club asked me to come up on the veranda and join him in a drink. This was a great way to spend a Sunday afternoon relaxing at a private club on one of the most beautiful beaches in the world. That only happened once. It might be interesting to note that the Outrigger Canoe is now a high rise hotel; however, at that time it was a one story private club.

From Pearl Harbor main gate to Waikiki was about 10 to 11 miles, and at that time about the only way to get there was in a taxicab. The cabs would fill up with sailors headed into town to get away from the mess at Pearl. The last return trip to Pearl Harbor from Honolulu was at 5:00 p.m. from the YMCA. The cabs would line up there with their Hawaiian drivers all hollering "Pa-laba" which didn't mean anything to me until the cabs started to fill up with sailors, so I jumped right in too.

One Sunday a sailor I rode into town with said that we should go ride the bus over the Pali. Not knowing what he was talking about, I went along and it was quite an experience. The bus was an old converted truck with the passenger section open on all sides and a canvas top with fringe all around.

Since the weather was so warm it was ideal for seeing out as we drove along. The road was the Nuuanu Pali Road, and it was a two-lane road with all kinds of twists and turns. This road, by the way, is now a four-lane freeway.

When we reached the Pali, the view was beautiful looking down over Honolulu and equally as beautiful overlooking Kaneohe Bay. It was breathtaking and I had never seen anything as pretty.

At 1207 feet, Nuuanu Pali is a peak overlooking Honolulu and Kaneohe Bay, and it gives one a chance to really appreciate the beauty of the islands. Looking out one sees the deep blue of the ocean outlined by the light blue of the sky, and as the water comes closer to the island it turns light blue and then green. As the water becomes shallow, the green fades into the white of the sandy beach. The beauty and tranquility of this sight confirms the fact that not all experiences in World War II were ugly and depressing.

From the Pali, we went down the Kaneohe side of the mountain and followed a road next to the beach, until we came to an outdoor restaurant. There, my friend introduced me to mahi-mahi fish and it turned out to be one of my favorite fish dishes. Of course other Sundays were spent sight-seeing around Honolulu and Waikiki, looking at the big hotels, like the Royal Hawaiian and the Moana, the Waikiki Aquarium and Fort De Russy.

During the first part of my stay in Hawaii, we were all worried about a return of the Japanese fleet. However, as days passed we began to feel a little more secure, and by the end of December no longer worried about a return attack. Here we were not battling the Japanese, but we sure had to battle the mosquitoes. Since December 7th, the mosquito abatement program ceased to operate, and when the oil was removed from the water in the harbor, the mosquitos were back in force making sleeping difficult.

Looking out over the harbor each morning, seeing all of the damaged battleships did not give me any confidence in our ability to win the Pacific war.

3

Southwest Pacific

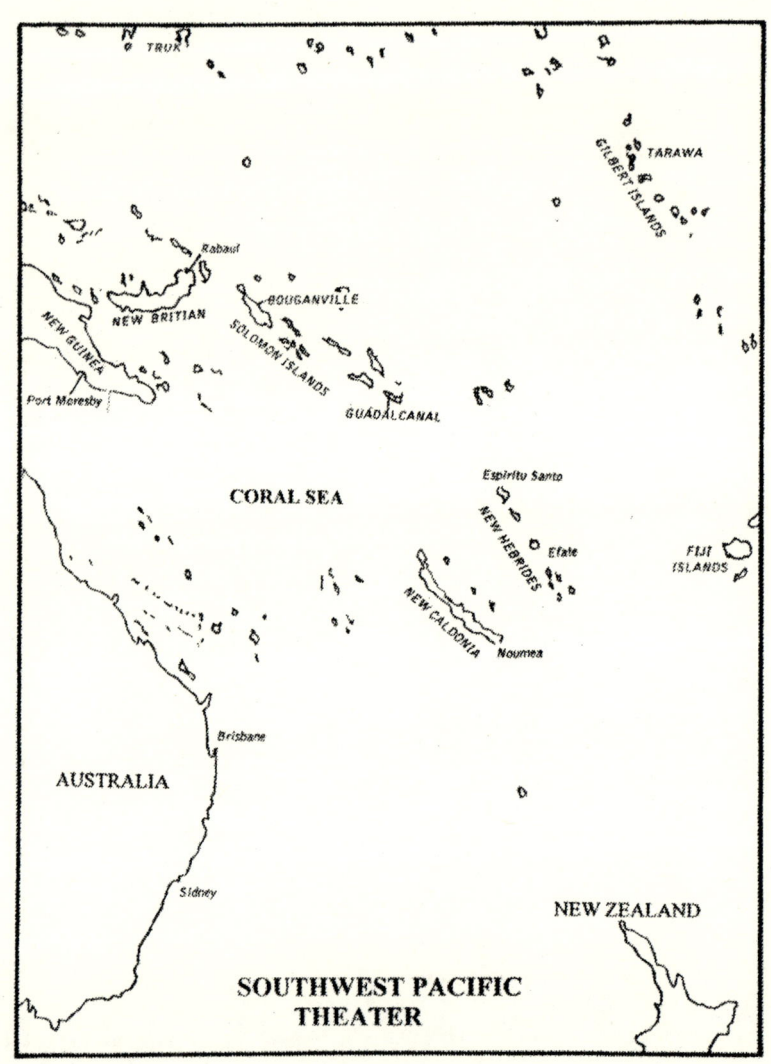

TRUK

TARAWA
GILBERT ISLANDS

Rabaul
NEW BRITIAN
BOUGANVILLE
NEW GUINEA
SOLOMON ISLANDS
Port Moresby
GUADALCANAL

Espiritu Santo
CORAL SEA
NEW HEBRIDES
Efate
FIJI
ISLANDS

NEW CALDONIA
Noumea

Brisbane

AUSTRALIA

Sidney

NEW ZEALAND

SOUTHWEST PACIFIC
THEATER

By the latter part of January 1942, I had been working with the maintenance crew of the *Whitney* for over a month and a half. As there were no further attacks on Pearl Harbor; any fears that were experienced when first arriving were now gone. Then Admiral William Halsey's Task Force 8 (TF8) returned to Pear Harbor from the Central Pacific where they had been conducting raids on the Marshall and Gilbert Islands. These ships were only here to take on more ammunition and fuel and they would soon be leaving again for more action. Knowing that my time here was limited waiting for the return of the destroyers, fear again returned with the expectation of being assigned to a front line ship.

No sooner had they arrived, than orders came in transferring me to the *USS Aylwin (DD355)* for duty. The *Aylwin* was built in 1935 and was one of eight *Farragut* class destroyers. These ships were the first destroyers to have dual-purpose five-inch guns installed. Dual-purpose means that they could be used to fire on air targets as well as surface targets. This class of destroyers had only three fire rooms, where most of the destroyers built afterwards had four. The smokestacks on the *Farragut* class ships had a small stack forward for one fire room and a larger stack aft for two fire rooms.

Since we only had three fire rooms, we did not consume as much fuel as the later destroyer types. This made our type of destroyer very much in demand for assignment with the fast carrier task forces since we did not have to be refueled as often.

After receiving orders, I then had to pack my sea bag, and report to the quarterdeck. There I picked up my orders and got a boat ride to my new ship. After the boat ride across the harbor, we came alongside and I went up the accommodation ladder to the quarterdeck where I reported to the officer of the deck. He had the boatswain of the watch take me below to the crew's quarters. There the boatswain showed me where to stow my gear and then he told me that my sleeping space was a hammock slung from beams in the overhead in the mess hall! This was a noisy place, even at night, because the men getting up to relieve the watch would come to the mess hall to get coffee and would be joking and talking.

* Photo courtesy of the United States Naval Institute

USS Aylwin DD355

When I arrived aboard, the ship was in the process of replenishing its stores, and after the process was completed we were ordered to get underway. The word was passed by the boatswain, "Make all preparations for getting underway."

The engineering department had to light off all boilers and man the machinery in the engine room. The deck department had to single up all lines securing the ship to the next one.

The captain on the bridge ordered all lines taken in except the spring line. He then ordered, ahead on port engine, until the bow started to move in and the stern move away from the next ship alongside. He then stopped the engines and had the last line taken in, and then backed both engines until the ship was clear of the others. He then ordered both engines ahead, and proceeded out the channel to the ocean.

Swinging in a hammock only lasted a few weeks until the chief boatswains mate moved me to a bunk on one side of the mess hall. It was the top bunk, and there was just barely enough room to squeeze in between the bunk surface and a large cable junction box on the overhead right above this bunk. It was all right until I had a dream one night, sat up, and really banged my head.

My service jacket indicated that I was a *radio striker*, and it also said *qualified radar*. However, there was no room in the radio shack for another radio striker, nor was there any radar on board. Therefore, I was assigned to stand watches with a five-inch gun crew, and my battle station was on #2 five-inch gun mount.

My job was powder handler which meant I had to take the powder can that came up on a hoist and drop it in the gun tray just ahead of the loading spade. One of the other men had the job of loading the five inch projectile ahead of the powder can.

While underway at sea, we stood watch at our assigned stations. As we were now at war, regulations stated that we were to maintain a State of Readiness III that required that we stand a four-hour watch and then had eight hours off. If we stood the eight to twelve watch in the morning, then we would stand the eight to twelve again in the evening.

We would keep this schedule for a week and then on Saturday we would *dog-the-watch*, which means that the four to eight watch in the afternoon would be broken up into two watches, four to six and six to eight. If we had been standing the eight to twelve, we would now be standing the four to eight for the next week, and the week after that it would the twelve to four. At first glance it looks like we should have been able to work in some uninterrupted sleep while not on watch. However, the most difficult time to detect submarine periscopes was just before sunrise and just after sunset. Therefore, we manned battle stations at general quarters (GQ) from an hour before sunrise until sunrise, and from sunset, until an hour after.

This made getting any sleep difficult. During daylight hours we were not supposed to sleep as there was daily work to be done during the morning and the afternoon watches by those not on watch. One of the daily activities was to practice on the five inch loading machine. This machine was located on the boat deck, one deck above the main deck. About mid morning the boatswain mate of the watch would pass the word for the five-inch gun crews to lay up to the loading machine for loading drills. This machine was built with a breach and tray similar to the ones on the five-inch guns.

There were dummy powder cans and dummy projectiles that were used to simulate the loading of the guns. We did this drill so often, it seemed that we could do it in our sleep, and we wondered why we had to keep doing it. We were soon to find out why.

The *Aylwin* had two five-inch guns mounted forward of the bridge, and two mounts aft of the after stack. The two mounts forward were equipped with splash shields which were open at the back, and the two guns aft were completely in the open. No matter which gun was manned, the crew on watch was always in the fresh air.

This made standing watches on the guns a pleasant way to spend four hours during daylight hours. At night, it was a different matter. In the past, having never had to stay up at night for four hours, made staying awake difficult for me. Each watch crew had a third class gunner's mate as the gun captain, and he was good at keeping us on our toes.

I had never drunk coffee before but soon found it necessary to stay awake. Standing watch at night, on one of the forward gun mounts, was a nice experience.

All of the ships were traveling with all outside lights off (darken ship) and we soon became adapted to seeing in the dark.

We could go forward on the fo'c'sle deck to the bow and look down at the bow wake which was phosphorescent. It was a beautiful sight when we could look over at the other ships and see their bow wakes. The weather was getting warmer and there was always a nice breeze blowing making things very comfortable.

These were pleasant sailing days, heading south before we came in to the forward area combat zones.

My fear had once again subsided and I was beginning to feel that this was not such a bad experience, after all. I missed not being assigned to the radio shack, but I was beginning to know the fellows on the gun crew. These men were a little rough around the edges, but most of them were good friends and we worked well together. I made daily trips to the radio shack to let the first class radioman know that I was ready to stand watches in the radio room.

Enroute to the South Pacific, we crossed the equator and those of us who had never been south before were called *Polly Wogs*, and we had to be initiated into the realm of *Neptune Rex*.

It was quite a ceremony. All of the sailors who had been across the equator before were called *Shellbacks*. First, we had our hair cut off, and then they put some kind of gooey substance all over our body. Next, they had set up a long canvas tube on the deck, and they had a fire hose at the far end shooting a powerful stream of salt water down the tube. We had to crawl through the tube against this high pressure water coming from a nozzle. When we managed to get through that, there was a long line of sailors on either side of us, and they all had wooden paddles and each one gave us a good whack as we ran down the line. Going up against the fire hose washed off most of the gooey mess, and we were now all qualified *Shellbacks*.

One morning, after we had been sailing for about a week and a half, we were called to general quarters at about 1030 hours.

There were several ships on the horizon and they were identified as U.S. Navy ships of Task Force 11. The *Aylwin* received orders to simulate a torpedo attack on the ships on the horizon with two other destroyers.

As we steamed to the attack at flank speed (maximum speed), the situation on the bridge became somewhat confused. There were two torpedo directors, one on the port wing of the bridge and the other on the starboard wing. At GQ, the torpedo director was manned by an ensign.

When the ship reached the point in the attack for the simulated launching of torpedo, the ensign gave the order to launch torpedo #1.

The torpedo was actually launched by the first class torpedoman, who was on the mount. All hell broke loose on the bridge, as the captain demanded to know who launched the torpedo. He also had to get on the TBS (ship to ship radio) and warn the ships in TF 11, that a fish was on its way and they should take evasive action. The next day, the destroyer division commander, who was on board the *Aylwin*, held a court of inquiry and the blame was laid on the first class torpedoman. This was my initiation into the system in the Navy, where officers protected their own.

This ensign was one of three ensigns who were on board the *Aylwin* on Sunday morning, December 7th, and they got the ship underway and out of Pearl Harbor safely.

It was obvious that the court did not want to enter a bad mark on his record that already had a commendation for his action on December 7th.

On the trip southwest our communication officer was looking for a librarian to keep track of all of the books. I volunteered, as that would give me a chance to pick out good books to read. Our library was located in the crew's mess hall. This was a job I kept until I left the ship in 1944.

Later that morning, we joined up with the *USS Lexington CV2* (one of our largest aircraft carriers) and other ships of Task Force 11 and headed for the Coral Sea. The Task Force was scheduled to head north and launch an air attack against the Japanese who had established a Naval operating base at Rabaul, New Britain. Now that we were in company with a carrier, the activity of the ships increased considerably. The *Lexington* conducted air operations daily while we were underway for Rabul.

* Photo courtesy of U.S. Navy Department -Naval Historical Center

USS Lexington CV2

Before dawn each morning, the *Lexington* would launch scout planes. These were type SBD aircraft (Scout Bomber Douglas).

They were dive-bombers built by Douglas Aircraft Corporation, and without a bomb load they were also used as scout planes. Navy crews named them *Dauntless*.

The task force commander, Vice Admiral Wilson Brown, kept scout planes in the air during daylight while in the forward combat area.

Air operations were always exciting to witness. Whenever a carrier is about to carry out flight operations, it will hoist the F (FOX) flag about half way up to the yardarm. On all of the other ships, a signalman on the bridge will call out to the Officer-of-the-Deck, "FOX is at the dip!"

When all ships have FOX at the dip, the carrier raises the flag all

41

of the way up to the yardarm (two blocking). When all ships have the flag two blocked, the carrier then hauls the flag down. This is a silent signal to all ships to execute a change of course into the wind.

The carrier turns into the wind and starts increasing speed to 32 knots (36.6mph). All ships would readjust their positions so that they were in the same relative position around the carrier on this new course, and these maneuvers by destroyers were carried out at their maximum speed available. The plane handling crews on the flight deck would move all of the planes to the after part of the flight deck, and then spot the planes to be launched as far back as possible. The planes spotted for take off would rev up their engines, and at the signal from the air officer, the brakes would be released and the plane would lurch forward starting its roll for take off.

* Photo courtesy of U.S. Navy Department -Naval Historical Center

SBD1

The SBDs used for scouting did not have a bomb attached when functioning as a scout plane, since maximum cruising range was desired. When they carried a bomb, they would reach airborne speed before they would clear the forward edge of the flight deck, and they would then drop a few feet before starting their climb. The *Lex* also carried TBD planes (Torpedo Bomber Douglas), and the flight crews called them *Devastators*. When the TBD's took off fully loaded, they would drop almost to the water before they would start their climb for altitude.

* Photo courtesy of U.S. Navy Department -Naval Historical Center

TBD Bomber

Landing operations were also exciting to watch. The carrier would again turn into the wind and increase to maximum speed. The plane handling crews would move all of the planes on flight deck all the way forward.

The aircraft would fly in a counter clockwise pattern to the port (left) side of the carrier and one at a time, a pilot would decrease altitude until he was just a little above flight deck, and start his approach to the rear of the flight deck.

At the rear edge of the flight deck on the port side, there was a Landing Signal Officer (LSO) to guide the pilots to a safe landing. The LSO had large paddles in either hand, and he would use them to signal the pilot. When a plane was ready to touch down, the pilot would lower his tail-hook. This hook was on an arm about two feet long, and it would catch on one of several steel cables that were stretched across the flight deck, held up about one foot off of the flight deck. These cables were attached to large springs at either end. When the hook caught, the cable would stop the plane in fifteen to twenty feet.

The U.S. Navy carriers also had a squadron of fighter planes on board. These were F4Fs where the first F stood for fighter, the 4 was the model, and the last F was for Grunman, Aircraft Corporation.

* Photo courtesy of U.S. Navy Department -Naval Historical Center

F4F Fighter

Fighter planes do not carry very much fuel and after several high-speed maneuvers they need to be recovered so they can be refueled. If the fighters were to escort the bombers on a long flight to a target, they would use belly-tanks to have enough fuel for the round trip.

They would cruise to the target using the belly-tank, and if they encountered enemy fighters, would drop those tanks and go to internal fuel tanks.

We had to go alongside the *Lexington* one morning and before we got alongside, our executive officer had the word passed that all hands topside had to shift into undress whites. We all got grumpy but went ahead and changed. When we got alongside, all of the sailors on the carrier were in dungarees. Even the ones on the bridge where the admiral was were in dungarees! Several months later when I was going to radar school at Pearl Harbor, I ran across a radioman from the carrier, and asked him how they got to wear dungarees on the flag-bridge when the admiral was present.

He said that when the war first started the radioman who took messages up to the flag bridge had to be in undress whites. One day when the man in undress whites was not in the radio shack, an urgent message came in, so one of the men in dungarees took the message up to the bridge. When he got there, the officer of the deck started giving him hell for coming to the bridge in dungarees. The admiral turned around, took a look at the radioman and said, "What's the matter?"

The OOD said, "This man is in dungarees."

The admiral said, "They are clean aren't they?"

The radioman I was talking to said that was the end of undress whites while underway at sea.

Early in the morning 20 February 1942, as the task force was just east of Bougainville in the Solomon chain, we were to scout out the Japanese forces at Rabaul on New Britain and Lea in New Guinea.

The *Lexington* launched several SBDs to scout to the north and some F4Fs to fly Combat Air Patrol (CAP). The function of the CAP was to fly a pattern above the carrier and be ready to protect the carrier from enemy planes. Mid-morning the *Lex's* air search radar picked up unidentified contact (bogie) and she turned into the wind to launch more CAP planes. All of the ships in TF11 went to general quarters (GQ).

On the *Lexington* Fighter Director Officer (FDO) vectored the CAP to intercept the contact. The CAP found the contact to be a

Japanese flying boat scout plane that we called *Mavis*. The CAP quickly shot it down, but not before it radioed Rabul that a large American task force was in the area.

Later another *Mavis* was picked up by the *Lex's* radar, and the CAP quickly shot it down. Just before noon we secured from GQ and had lunch.

At 1540 hours (2:40 p.m.), the *Lexington* again picked up several bogies, and the CAP was vectored to intercept. They reported that the contact was a formation of nine twin-engine bombers, which we called Betty. The CAP managed to shoot down seven and the other two were damaged, but managed to get away. About an hour later radar reported another raid approaching. The *Lex* again hoisted FOX flag, launched a CAP and we all went to GQ. The contact faded from the radar screen so the FDO vectored the planes in the general direction of the contact. Lt. Edward "Butch" O'Hare and his wingman sighted another formation of eight Betty bombers and he climbed for altitude and tested their guns. The wingman's guns failed to fire so Butch attacked the formation by himself.

As he started his attack, they all came into or view and we were spellbound to see him shooting down one after another. He was able to shoot down six of the raid, and when the last two approached, all of the ships started to fire antiaircraft guns.

Soon some bombs started to fall between the *Lex* and the *Alywin*. When I saw them falling, I guess I was in a state of shock because I couldn't move.

Our gun captain hollered at me and had to come over and give me a good kick. We finally got the gun in action, and I finally understood why we had so many loading drills.

I was so scared that I couldn't even think about what we were doing, but I managed to do the loading job anyway. All I could think about was how did I ever get in combat so soon, while all of my friends were safe, back in the states going to school. I finally snapped out of my daze when the attack retired and we ceased fire.

Thinking about what we had been through after we secured from GQ, I came to the conclusion that it had not been too bad and no one on board was hurt. There was a lot of action and noise as five-inch guns make very loud noise when they are fired and we were right next to one. We fired over 300 rounds of 5 inch projectiles during the attack. The *Aylwin* shot down one plane that tried to crash dive on the destroyer *Bagley* and it crashed well astern of the *Bagley*.

It was an exciting experience seeing the dive-bombers taking off and then the fighters, and then seeing Butch shoot down so many planes in such a short time. In four minutes Butch had become the Navy's first WWII ace, and he received the Medal of Honor. The airport in Chicago is named after Butch, the O'Hare International Airport. This attack was called Air Action off Bouganville.

During the action we had been plane guard for the *Lexington* during air operations. The plane guard is stationed about 500 yards behind the carrier and to her starboard. This gives us a good view of the flight deck and also a good view of the landing operations. The function of the plane guard destroyer is to pick up the pilot and crew of any plane that crashes, or can't make it to the flight deck and lands in the water.

Of course, the destroyer has to be able to make as many knots as the carrier during air operations. The next two weeks TF11 conducted search operations and refueling, and then on 6 March we had a rendezvous with TF17 which had been operating in the Southwest Pacific. TF17 was made up of the carrier *Yorktown* and her escorting cruises and destroyers.

These two task forces combined and became TF11 under the command of Admiral Fletcher. The task force was to proceed to the south of New Guinea and launch an air strike over the mountain range to Lea and Salamaua, New Guinea.

The *Aylwin* again served in the antisubmarine screen for the task force, and as plane guard for the *Lex* during air operations. During these carrier raids our only significant experience was being plane guard during air operations. The Japanese did not mount any further air raids on our task force on this cruise.

* Photo courtesy of U.S. Navy Department -Naval Historical Center

USS Yorktown CV-5

While February and March are winter months back home, they are summer months in areas south of the equator. As we were enjoying warm weather we took the opportunity to sun bathe when not on watch.

The second class gunners mate, who was gun captain on five inch mount number two, would go up to the deck near his gun and strip down naked to sun bathe. One of the Chief petty officers told him that if he got his penis or testicles sunburned, he would become sterile.

The next afternoon, he showed up with a sweat sock over his organs. We all had a good laugh because he would believe anything that a chief would tell him. We had a radio striker in the radio shack, and one afternoon he went back to sunbathe on the fantail and he fell asleep.

When he looked like a ripe apple, someone woke him up and was he ever in pain. After a couple of days, when the redness went down, he had small white dots all over his chest. These spots never did go away.

The *Aylwin* was having trouble keeping up with the *Lexington*. We were experiencing leaks in some of the super heat tubes in the boilers. Without super heated steam, a destroyer cannot make maximum speed. This condition was reported to the task force commander, and we soon received orders to proceed to Pearl Harbor Navy Yard for repairs. We escorted the *Lexington* back to Pearl arriving on 26 March 1942.

While at Pearl Harbor, the Navy yard installed our first air search radar, a model SC. Since this was not the same type that we had studied in the radar class, I needed to be on board to watch all of the installation instead of going on liberty to Honolulu.

When the repairs to the boilers were completed, and the new SC radar installed, we got underway and cleared the harbor bound for the Southwest Pacific, again. Now that we had radar on board, I was taken off the gun crew and assigned to training the radar operators and standing watch in the radio shack.

When I was standing watches on the gun crew, I had started smoking cigarettes. Since we didn't have anything to do on gun watch other than be ready set up to fire on short notice, we would sit around and tell stories. Most of the gun crew smoked. When they would light up, someone would offer me a cigarette.

Since a pack cost only 5 cents at the ship's store, I started buying my own and that started my tobacco habit that was to last 29 years.

When I moved to the radio shack to stand watch, I tried smoking cigarettes, but it was a losing effort. There was no air conditioning in the radio shack, and at night, the air in the radio shack was still. When sitting, copying the broadcast code from Pearl Harbor on the typewriter, the smoke from the end of a cigarette would slowly rise up and get caught in my eye sockets. Pretty soon my eyes would start to burn and I would not be able to see what I was typing. The other radiomen already knew this and they all had switched to smoking pipes. This way the smoke was kept away from the eyes, so I switched to a pipe also.

The new SC radar had a rotating bedspring antenna mounted on top of the main mast. This mast was about 50 feet tall and there was a vertical ladder up the forward side. Once a week, I had to climb the mast to service the radar antenna.

To work on anything on the mast required wearing a safety belt which was made of stiff canvas with a large ring on either side just above the hips. A line attached to one ring, and before starting any work, we were required to pass the line around the mast or the ladder and secure it to the other large ring. After finishing the work on the antenna, I stayed for a while and looked around at the ocean and down at the ship. As the ship would roll, I could look straight down and see nothing but water with the ship off to my right or left. From this lofty point it was obvious that a destroyer was a very narrow ship and it would be very difficult for any aircraft to hit it with a bomb.

This observation relieved most of the fear that I had experienced during the 20 February 1942 air attack. From this point on, I never worried about being hit from horizontal bombers. Not having seen dive-bombers and torpedo-planes in action yet, I didn't have any feeling about them.

The distance from Pearl Harbor to the Coral Sea is about 3,150 miles, and traveling at our cruising speed of 15 knots takes about 9 days to arrive in the Coral Sea to rejoin TF11.

This was an uneventful trip and became boring after a few days just standing watches, going to battle stations every morning and evening, and doing routine work during the day.

It did provide me time to train new radar operators and learn more about the new equipment. This period also gave me a chance to get to know the radiomen where I was standing watch.

My first memorable experience occurred on a night watch when radioman first class Olsen told me to take the coffee pot down to the galley and get water so we could make a fresh pot. When I got to the galley, the inside of the pot was so caked with build up of coffee deposits, that I decided to clean it out.

When I brought it back with fresh water Olsen gave me hell saying that it had taken them months to build up the deposits. He said that the deposit gave the coffee a real good taste. Of course he was kidding, but I didn't know it at the time. As I was to find out as time went by, there was a lot of kidding going on all over the ship, and at this time I was the only reservist on board, so I received a lot. When one gets kidded on board, you know that the crew is beginning to accept you.

One morning when I was not on watch, I got called up to the radio shack. When I arrived, I was assigned to a working party to clear out our radio storage area.

This area was about four feet by eight feet and it had an expanded metal front and a gate. We were told that this space was needed for a brig (a jail cell in civilian life).

It turned out that one of the new sailors was homosexual, and they needed to isolate him. I couldn't figure that out as he didn't pose a threat to any of us, but then I was told that it was to protect him from the rest of us straight guys. We had a number of fellows who were real macho and they would have done him in, I'm sure.

4

Coral Sea

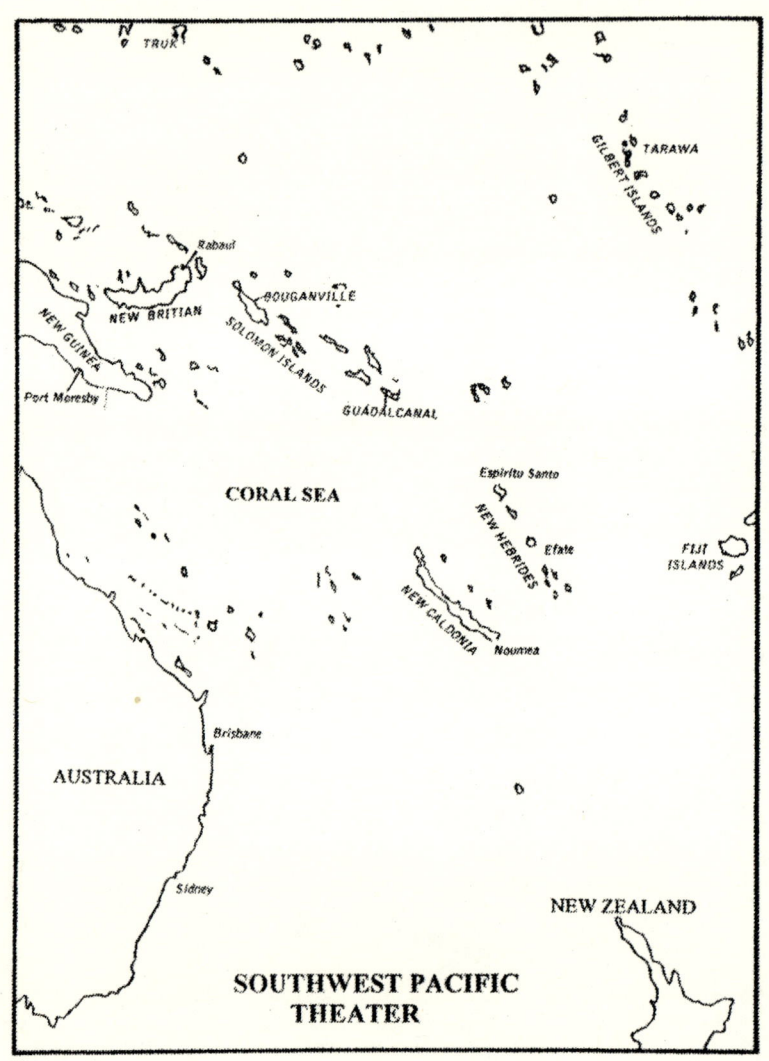

TRUK

TARAWA

GILBERT ISLANDS

Rabaul

NEW BRITIAN

BOUGANVILLE

NEW GUINEA

SOLOMON ISLANDS

Port Moresby

GUADALCANAL

Espiritu Santo

CORAL SEA

NEW HEBRIDES

Efate

FIJI ISLANDS

NEW CALEDONIA

Noumea

Brisbane

AUSTRALIA

Sidney

NEW ZEALAND

SOUTHWEST PACIFIC
THEATER

Before leaving Pearl Harbor on 17 April 1942, we were told the Japanese planned to attack and take over Port Moresby in Papua, New Guinea and Tulagi Island in the Solomon chain, during early May.

This would cut off the United States' lines of communication with Australia. Admiral Nimitz, Commander in Chief Pacific and Admiral King, Chief of Naval Operations, met in San Francisco and decided that we had to stop the Japanese advance to the south. Admiral Nimitz ordered the carriers *Lexington* (CV-2) and *Yorktown* (CV-5) to proceed to a rendezvous point in the Coral Sea and combine task forces to attack any Japanese forces in the area of Port Moresby, and attack any Japanese amphibious operations in the area. Admiral Halsey's TF 12 was returning to Pearl Harbor after delivering the B-25 raid on Tokyo, but they would not be able to make it to Pearl, and then down to the Coral Sea in time to join TF 11 and TF 17 at the rendezvous point by 1 May.

The trip back to the Coral Sea was uneventful, and we stood watches and observed the aircraft operations on the *Lexington*. It did give me a chance to continue training radar operators, which we did on a daily basis. Getting up in the middle of the night to stand my watch was something that was hard to get used to. At first, I had the tendency to roll over and go back to sleep when getting a call to get up. I soon overcame that tendency when I saw the Chief Boatswain Mate Hackler come back to make a second call on another man. The Chief reached in and lifted that man out of his bunk and dropped him on the steel deck.

That was enough to make me get up after the first call. All of the spaces on the ship had general quarters alarms which were Klaxton horns. When general quarters was called, these horns would give off a rasping sound — braz-braz-braz — etc.

It was loud enough to wake up anyone, and after our experiences in the February air attack off Bougainville, we would all roll out of our bunks, grab our pants and our life jackets, and head for our battle stations on the run.

My new battle station was on the operating console of the air search radar that was located in the chart house just below the bridge deck. There was also another radar operator by the name of Johnson assigned to this battle station. He became the senior operator and was my right hand man in the repair and maintenance of the radar systems on board. We always had two operators during a four-hour watch and they would take turns watching the oscilloscope for an echo (contact). Johnson and I did the same thing during general quarters.

On 1 May, we made a rendezvous with TF 17 and the *Yorktown* in the northern part of the Coral Sea. TF 17 was fueling from the *Neosho* (AO-7), one of our fleet tankers, and then TF 11 and the *Lexington* started refueling. Refueling at sea takes quite a bit of time as only two ships can refuel at once from the tanker. The process usually takes more than one day, with a number of combat ships in the task force to be refueled.

The task force commander always wants his ships topped off with fuel before going into battle. The larger ships, cruisers and carriers, can carry enough fuel to run a maximum speed for several days, but destroyers can only make maximum speed for just a little over a day, therefore destroyers are topped off first.

Fueling at sea is an interesting operation to witness. We would approach the tanker from astern on the same course and then go alongside of the tanker and match the tanker's speed. The tanker crew would throw over a messenger line which we would pull aboard. Attached to the small messenger line was a larger line, which we pulled aboard, and attached to that larger line would be the fueling hose. The fuel hose would then be pulled aboard and placed into a large fueling pipe in the main deck that was connected to our fuel tanks.

The signal was then given to the tanker, and they would start pumping oil. Men from our engineering department had to watch the oil level in each tank to make sure we didn't overfill. If this occurred, we would end up with heavy black oil all over our deck.

Keeping the destroyer at just the right distance from the tanker was a tricky operation as the water between the two ships was forced to flow faster than the water on our outboard side. This decreased the pressure between the two ships, and tended to force us into the tanker. Our captain was at the con of our ship, and he would be in the wing of the bridge constantly watching the distance between the tanker and our ship, and giving orders to the helmsman to steer our ship to stay at just the right separation.

When tanks were full, we would signal the tanker and they would stop the flow of oil and recover their hoses and lines. We would then increase speed and pull away from the tanker, and the next ship in line would go alongside the tanker to be topped off.

* Photo courtesy of U.S. Navy Department -Naval Historical Center

Fueling at Sea from a Tanker

On 3 May, we received a message that the Japanese were invading Tulagi Island in the Solomon chain. We ceased fueling operations, and headed toward Tulagi at 24 knots.

On 4 May, the *Lexington's* planes raided this landing operation and forced it to retreat after landing only a few troops. Later that day, we rejoined TF 17 that had been separated from TF 11 during fueling operations. Since the *Yorktown* did not have as many destroyers for ASW screen and anti-aircraft screen, we were ordered to join the screening vessels for the *Yorktown*. We still did not know where the Japanese carriers were located. We did have intelligence information that there should be two fleet carriers to support the invasions of Tulagi and Port Moresby.

On 5 May, the *Yorktown's* CAP shot down a flying boat scout plane but we did not know if it was able to report our position. We were all getting excited waiting for something to break. We still had scout planes out from both carriers, but no contacts were reported. We were scanning the sky continuously with our air search radar, but our only contacts were identified as friendly.

At 19 years old, I was typically in love with speed as were most young men. Being on a destroyer was just the place to be to satisfy this appetite. When a carrier was going to turn into the wind to carry out flight operations, the destroyer would have to go to a flank speed of 36 knots to get to their screening position on the new course. We would be steaming along at standard speed (15 knots) and when air operations were about to take place, the fox flag would go up to the dip position and we would go to flank speed. The sudden acceleration and course change to maneuver to our new position as plane guard would cause the stern deck of the *Aylwin* to dig down into the water and flood the fantail deck. Whenever there were men on the fantail and someone saw the fox flag go up, he would yell, "Fox at the dip." Everyone on the fantail deck would run for cover of the after deckhouse. Destroyers were real hot rods when it came accelerating. We had 42,000 shaft horsepower, and when speed was increased to flank, we could feel the whole stern of the ship begin to vibrate, as the power of the screws was biting into the water. It was invigorating to feel so much power being applied.

All day long we had scout planes and CAP in the air and they had to land and be refueled periodically, so the activity during the day was at a high level.

The ships of both of our task forces were joined into a single task force under Admiral Jack Fletcher and it was named Task Force 17. On 6 May 1942, TF 17 was sighted by a Japanese scout plane flying out of Rabaul. Our scout planes had not sighted any Japanese ships due to their carriers being hidden by a large area of storm clouds. During this day and during the night of 6 May, TF 17 and the Japanese task force came within 100 miles of each other with no contacts made.

When the *Yorktown* and her screening ships had finished fueling, the *Neosho* and the *Sims* were ordered to head to the south part of the Coral Sea to be clear of any action that was to take place.

On 7 May 1942 before dawn, the *Aylwin* went to general quarters, and at 8:17 a.m. the *Yorktown* CAP shot down a Japanese float scout plane from one of their cruisers. At 8:40 a.m., one of our scout planes reported sighting two Japanese carriers to the north of our position.

About 10:15 a.m., Admiral Fletcher ordered a strike and both carriers launched a 93 plane attack against the ships reported by our scout plane. About a half an hour later, the scout plane was recovered and it was discovered that the pilot had made an error in the coded message reporting two carriers. What he should have reported was seeing a small carrier and a cruiser.

At about this same time, the Japanese launched a 73 plane attack against, what their scout plane identified as, the U.S. Task Force. When the Japanese raid found the ships reported by their scout plane, they turned out to be the *Neosho* and *Sims*. Having no other targets all 73 planes made attacks on the *Neosho* and *Sims*. The *Sims* put up a good fight but was soon sunk.

The *Neosho* was badly damaged but refused to sink. Survivors were picked up a few days later by one of our destroyers and the destroyer torpedoed the wreckage of the *Neosho* and sank it.

At a little after noon on 7 May, planes from TF 17 found the ships reported by our scout plane. One of the ships was the light carrier *Soho*, supporting amphibious landings at another location.

They had no other large carriers in sight, so they attacked and sank the *Soho* and some of the amphibious vessels.

In our radio shack, we were monitoring the reports from the pilots, and we were exhilarated at the success our planes were having, not knowing at that time that they had attacked a small carrier. We had been at general quarters since before dawn, and we were getting hungry so the captain ordered the cooks to go to the galley and bring food to all battle stations. Soon, the cooks arrived with large tubs — hot dogs in one and buns in the other. So we're having a picnic with hot dogs and buns while a battle is going on. So far, we had seen no Japanese planes. We were getting to feel very secure and enjoying all of the excitement; but, there is more to come.

At 4:00 p.m., a Japanese float scout plane sighted TF 17 and reported to the Japanese carriers. Admiral Hora, commander of the Japanese carrier force, launched an attack of 12 VAL dive-bombers and 17 KATE torpedo planes.

At about 6:00 p.m., we picked up these planes on our radar, and a short time later our CAP attacked the raid and broke it up before they got close enough for a strike against our carriers. The Japanese lost seven planes during this sortie.

Admiral Fletcher decided not to launch a large raid against their carriers as the distance was over 175 miles, and our returning planes would arrive back after dark. We finally secured from battle stations and had something to eat.

On 8 May, activity started early again with general quarters an hour before dawn and the carriers launching scout planes and CAP fighters.

After sunrise, we secured from general quarters and had breakfast. At about 8:15 a.m., before we had time to start any work, the *Lexington's* radar detected an aircraft at about 60 miles. The CAP was vectored out to the contact and they chased off another enemy float plane.

A short time later, our scout planes, which had been launched just before dawn, spotted the Japanese task force with the carriers *Shokaku* and *Zuikaku* about 175 miles east north east from our position. We went to general quarters again, and at about 9:00 a.m., the *Lexington* and the *Yorktown* launched a 73 plane raid against the Japanese carriers.

This was an exciting time as we watched both carriers launching planes, and the planes orbiting overhead waiting for the last plane to get airborne. When that occurred, they all took off toward the enemy carriers. At about that same time, the Japanese launched a 69 plane raid toward us. Both of the raids passed each other enroute to their targets without engagement because they were both intent on their target carriers.

At 11:00 a.m., the *Lexington's* radar picked up many bandits, and the CAP attacked. The CAP was so busy engaging the ZERO fighters that the VALs and KATEs got through.

Both the *Lexington* and the *Yorktown* started high speed maneuvers to dodge torpedos and bombs. The *Yorktown*, being somewhat smaller than the *Lexington*, was able to dodge the torpedos, but she did take a large bomb hit in the middle of the flight deck. The bomb penetrated the flight deck, and exploded down below.

The *Aylwin* was about 100 yards from the port side of the *Yorktown* during the attack, and the anti-aircraft by our five-inch guns hit a torpedo plane just before it dropped its bomb. It exploded in a huge ball of fire that destroyed the next plane in line.

While this was going on our captain, LCDR Phalen, was shooting a 50 caliber machine gun at the attacking planes.

Of course, he was never able to hit anything as the planes were out of range of his gun. But this action made the crew members really proud to be serving with him.

After he had his fun firing away, Destroyer Division Commander 2 who was aboard called to our captain, "George, come look at this!" He was talking about the Japanese torpedo planes dropping their torpedos at high speed and the torpedos would surface, and run true to their target. At that stage of the war, our aerial torpedos could only be dropped at a very slow speed.

My breathing was heavy and fast and my heartbeat was racing, but I did not experience the same fear I had had in February during the air attack off Bougainville. Knowing that a destroyer is a small target and that the main target was the carrier, I was not worrying much about our getting hit. We could not hear anything with all of our guns firing anti-aircraft shots, and with the wind blowing so hard as we were making flank speed.

Being so large, the *Lexington* was not able to maneuver quickly, and was under a torpedo and dive bomb attack. I looked over in time to see two KATEs each drop their torpedoes that hit the port side of the carrier.

She also took several bomb hits from VAL dive-bombers, and she started to list to port as several compartments were flooded. About the same time we took a near miss from a 550 lb. bomb that exploded in the water near our starboard side. It sounded like a large thud and threw water up on our decks, but we didn't slow down any and we kept firing.

The *Yorktown* had slowed considerably after the bomb hit, but their damage control party got things patched up. She was soon able to make good speed and recover planes.

The *Lexington's* damage control parties managed to flood starboard compartments and get the ship back on an even keel. They had some fires aboard but had extinguished them and she was recovering planes. One of the SBD Dauntless dive bombers came back with a big hole in its wing and, thankfully, we recovered the pilot and radioman after they landed the plane in the water.

At 12:45 p.m., the *Lexington* suffered a huge explosion deep inside of the ship when sparks from an emergency generator ignited gasoline fumes from a broken fuel line in a large closed compartment. Unfortunately, the damage control parties were not able to shut off the flow of gasoline and the fire became so large that they were unable to control it. I looked over and saw huge columns of smoke billowing up into the sky. She had now come to a complete stop and at 3:07 p.m. Captain Sherman gave the order to abandon ship.

* Photo courtesy of U.S. Navy Department -Naval Historical Center

Explosion On The Lexington

Our exhilaration of yesterday now turned into distress and grief. We were witnessing the loss of one of the largest aircraft carriers in the world, and one that was loved deeply by all who had served aboard her.

I was wondering how were we going to continue the fight with only the damaged *Yorktown*. The Japanese were not mounting another attack as far as we could see. We had no more contacts on our SC radar.

We were still at battle stations, and again we had hot dogs for lunch, as we watched the carrier burn and men going down lines to the water and waiting ships. It was a sad and depressing sight to see such a magnificent ship being destroyed. After several of the other escorting ships had picked up their load of survivors, we went in and picked up a large number of men.

After sunset the *Lex* was still burning and was giving away our position. Therefore, Admiral Fletcher ordered the destroyer *Phelps* to torpedo her. The *Phelps* ran in close and fired five torpedos, three of which exploded. A short time later the gallant lady rolled over and sank.

It was a sad day for all of us. We were walking around in stunned silence, not knowing what to think or to say. We had a feeling that we had lost the battle, but of course we did not know at that time what damage the Japanese task force had suffered. As far as we knew, they still had an undamaged carrier and were in a good situation to launch another attack.

This worried most of us and we were apprehensive about what was going to happen next. By late afternoon of 8 May, TF 17 was not in condition to carry on the battle.

We had lost the *Lexington*, *Neosho* and *Sims*. The *Yorktown* had suffered a large bomb hit, and she had expended all of the airborne tropedos. She could only muster eight fighters and fifteen dive bombers for an attack. Admiral Nimitz ordered Admiral Fletcher to retire from the Coral Sea and return to Pearl Harbor.

After the battle, we were all talking about what we had seen. Several sailors who had battle stations on the after guns told us what they had seen. The executive officer's battle station is at after con, out in the open, located on a platform behind the after stack. He is stationed there in case the bridge is hit and loses control. Witnesses said that when action started, he ran forward from his station to the wardroom.

The trip back to Pearl Harbor seemed to take longer than the trip down. We had about 37 officers and 92 enlisted men survivors from the *Lexington*, and with conditions crowded with just our crew of three hundred, the extra men made living a little tight. We all gave up clothing, blankets and toilet articles to the survivors.

We had to sleep in shifts, and most bunks were used all of the time. One of the survivors was an officer from Admiral Fitch's staff on the carrier. He was an intelligence officer who could read Japanese language and break their lower order codes. He came to the radio shack, and told us about the U.S. Navy breaking the Japanese codes. That the U.S. Navy had the capability to read their messages amazed us. This officer told us that our Navy knew the Japanese had two fleet carriers in the Coral Sea.

On 15 May, we entered Tongatabu harbor and transferred the survivors to the *Portland*. With all of the urgent activity in early 1942, I still carried the rating of apprentice seaman. I had been asked to help the sonarmen take care of the sonar submarine search system.

The principal of operation of this equipment was similar to that of radar. I had worked on these systems at Pearl Harbor in December and January. As we were approaching Pearl Harbor, our fathometer failed and I was asked to see if I could fix it. The fathometer measures the depth of the water under the ship using equipment similar to sonar. I obtained the instruction manual, and was trying to find the failure when the messenger from the bridge came down and said the captain wanted to see me on the bridge, immediately.

When I arrived on the bridge, he said that I was to get the fathometer fixed right away or he would break me. (To break a man means to reduce him in rate.) I said, "You can't do that."

He exploded and said, "What do you mean I can't do that?"

I said, "I am just an apprentice seaman."

The captain then turned to the officer-of-the-deck and said, "Get the executive officer up here, get the communication officer up here, get the chief yeoman up here." He then turned to me and said, "You stand right there." By this time I was beginning to sweat and to feel real nervous wondering what was going to happen.

When they all arrived he turned to them and said, "I am going to rate this man third class radioman today," then turning to me he said, "now I can break you if I want. Go fix my damned fathometer."

This is how I skipped two ratings to make third class petty officer.

Normally I would have to been advanced to seaman second class and then to seaman first class. Then after a period I could take the test for radioman third class and after passing that I would be a rated petty officer. I had already been standing watches in the radio shack so there was no change in my watch station. (A plan view of the radio shack is shown below.)

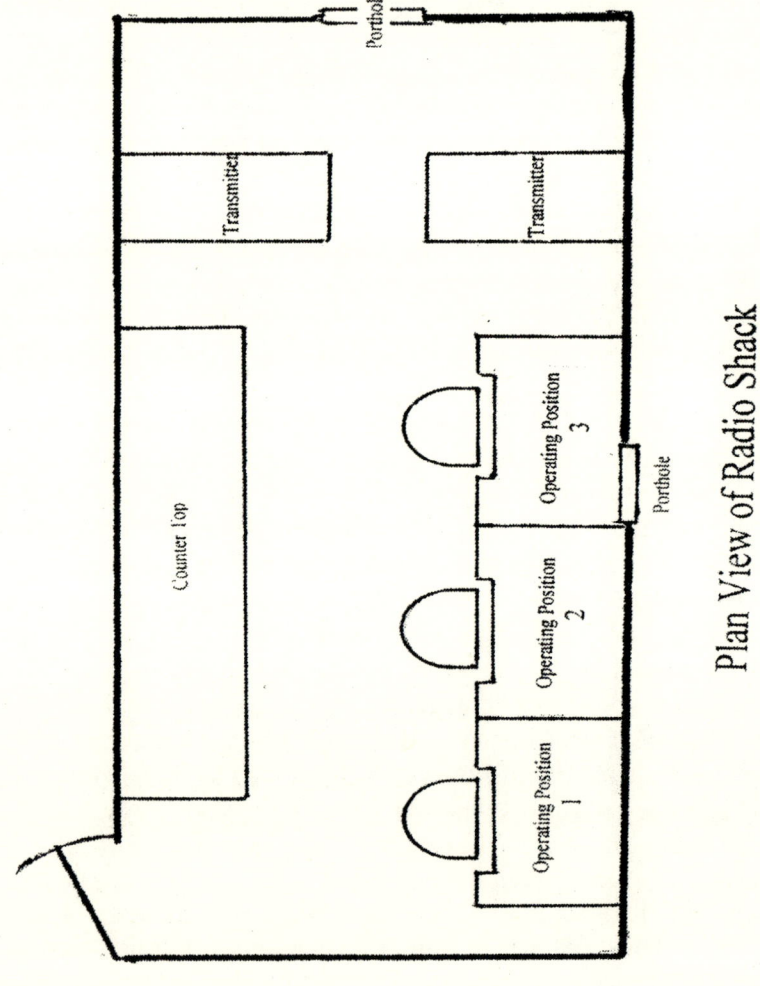

Plan View of Radio Shack

The radiomen standing watch in operating positions 1 and 2 were guarding emergency radio circuits that normally had no signals, unless we were going into battle and the enemy knew our location. When they knew our position, these circuits became alive and we had to guard them.

The radioman in operating position 3 copied a broadcast circuit from Hawaii. Broadcast means that Hawaii would send messages to all ships and stations and we had to copy these signals 24 hours a day.

Since we were in a condition of radio silence, we could not respond to indicate we had received the messages. They were in code and we had to break the first few lines to determine the addressee. If we were one of the addressees, a copy of the message would be delivered to one of the officers on the coding board. That officer would take the message into a locked room where the electric coding machine was located. He would decode the message and deliver it to the communications officer. We had three radiomen on each watch, two would be in the operating positions and one would run messages and relieve the man in position 3 every half hour. This set up resulted in two of us not being too busy on a night watch. On my watch, another radioman, Eldor Ulrich, and I would play blackjack for match sticks. At the end of a four-hour watch, neither of us would come away a consistent winner. This was just one way of staying awake at night. We had a radioman 2nd class who came from the *USS West Virginia* and after December 7th, he ended up on the *Aylwin*.

This man played a fiddle in his off hours, and he had a full beard. He appeared to be about 35 years old and he talked with a slow, southern drawl.

On the return trip from the Coral Sea, Admiral Fletcher issued an order that all beards had to be shaved off, and all men would have to be clean shaven from now on. There had been a number of bad facial burns during the battle. When this radioman shaved his beard and came to the radio shack, we didn't know him! He looked 10 years younger, but we still recognized his southern drawl.

Our radio shack had no air conditioning. At night, when we were at darken ship, both of our port holes had to be closed. That room sure did get hot and stuffy at night and we took turns going out on deck to get fresh air.

As a result of the near miss by one of the Japanese bombs, our damage control division found that some of the welded seams on the hull had split and we were taking on water. The engineering department had all of the pumps on the *Aylwin* working, even the emergency fire fighting pumps, and we were not able to keep up with the flooding.

During the trip back to Pearl Harbor, we had our fingers crossed hoping that we would make it to dry dock. We did make it and when we entered the harbor, we did not have to stop in West Loch and offload ammunition as was usually required. We headed straight into a dry dock and the Navy Yard workers came aboard to start repairing the leaks and other damage.

During the battle of the Coral Sea the U.S. Navy lost 543 men, and the Japanese Navy lost 1047 men. We lost a fleet carrier, a fleet oiler, and a destroyer. They lost a light carrier, a destroyer and several amphibious vessels.

We lost 66 aircraft. The Japanese lost 93.

The Japanese Navy also suffered heavy damage to their two large fleet carriers which returned to their navy yard in Japan for several months of repairs.

As a result of the Coral Sea action, the Japanese called off the amphibious landings at Port Moresby. This ended their southward expansion in the Southwest Pacific, and kept our lines of communication open to Australia. The damage to two of their large fleet carriers precluded their participation in the attack on Midway.

5

Midway

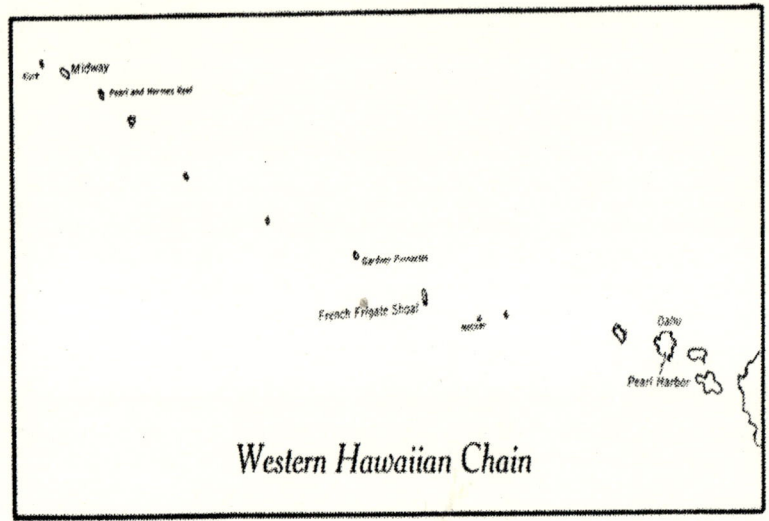

Western Hawaiian Chain

* The above map gives you an idea of the location of the Midway Islands with respect to Pearl Harbor. The following map shows the two islands and the lagoon of the atoll as they existed in 1942.

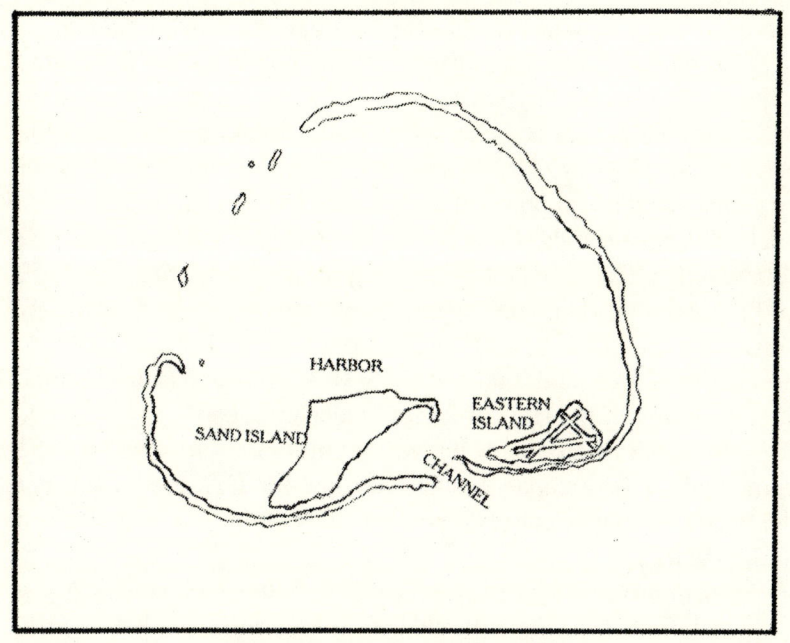

MIDWAY ATOLL

The airstrips at that time were located on Eastern Island, where as today they are located on Sand Island. Before I get into my experiences during the Battle of Midway, some background information is in order. In the entire history of naval warfare there have been few that compare to Midway. It ranks up there with the defeat of the Spanish Armada, Trafalgar and Jutland. Prior to the Midway action, the Japanese had free run in the Pacific and they seemed unstoppable. Military historian, John Keegan, has called the Battle of Midway, "as great a reversal of strategic fortune as the naval world has seen."

The reason that historians have attached so much importance to this battle, is that they consider it as the turning point of the war in the Pacific. This action at Midway was the last time that the Imperial

Japanese Navy conducted any offensive operation in the Pacific.

The Midway Islands are an unincorporated territory of the United States in the Central Pacific Ocean. They are located near the western end of the Hawaiian chain, with the large island of Hawaii at the eastern end. Midway is 1,300 miles west-north-west of Pearl Harbor on Oahu, and it is composed of a coral atoll 15 miles in circumference enclosing two islands, Eastern and Sand. The total land area is 2 square miles. The islands were claimed for the United States in 1859 and the name Midway dates from 1867, when they were formally annexed by the U.S. In 1903 President Theodore Roosevelt placed the control of the islands under the U.S. Navy and Sand Island became a relay station of the Hawaii-Luzon underwater cable.

Admiral Yamamoto, who was commander in chief of the combined fleets of Japan, wanted to draw the U.S. Fleets out into the Pacific so that he could crush them and continue to have free run in the Pacific.

Yamamoto cited the need for a decisive battle with the U.S. Navy early in the war, since Japan could not carry on any extended warfare, as they were lacking the required natural resources and industrial capability for prolonged operations.

He proposed to the Japanese high command, that he would conduct a diversion attack on Dutch Harbor, Alaska using a two carrier fleet. The following day he would conduct heavy aircraft raids on the Midway Atoll by his main fleet with four aircraft carriers. This would surely draw the American carrier fleet out of Pearl Harbor to protect Midway. The Japanese Naval High Command did not like the plan because Midway only had two square miles of land area that would be very hard to defend. They also did not like the plan because the supply lines to Midway would be so long and they would be vulnerable to submarine attacks. They were not in favor of the plan and did not want to approve it, but Yamamoto threatened to resign if he was not allowed to carry it out. So, they relented and Yamamoto had his way.

Against Yamamoto's 135 warships, Admiral Nimitz could only muster a total of 49 American warships. Admiral William Halsey and his TF 16, with the carriers *Enterprise* and *Hornet*, had been operating in the South West Pacific, so Admiral Nimitz ordered Halsey to make sure the Japanese saw his Task Force 16 down there and then return to Pearl Harbor at his maximum possible speed.

* Photo courtesy of U.S. Navy Department -Naval Historical Center

USS Enterprise

When Task Force 16 returned to Pearl from the South West Pacific, Halsey was sick and Nimitz ordered him to the hospital. Halsey suggested that Nimitz make Admiral Spruance head of TF 16 which Nimitz readily agreed to. The next day Task Force 16 got underway to the west. Task Force 17, under Admiral Fletcher with the *Yorktown*, was still in dry-dock undergoing urgent repairs, and would join up with TF 16 as soon as possible.

In Pearl Harbor Navy Yard, the *Aylwin* was in one dry dock and the *Yorktown* was in an adjacent dry dock. The Navy yard workers at Pearl Harbor worked as if someone had lit a fire under them to get the damage from the Coral Sea battle repaired. We knew that something big was going on because in the other dry dock the *Yorktown* workers were all over her like ants on food. The work on both ships went on 24 hours a day. The repairs to the *Aylwin* were completed in just over 24 hours, and we left the dry dock and headed out to sea. The *Yorktown* would leave her dock after another 36 hours and head out to sea again.

In the radio shack, we were wondering what the next action was going to be and what the big hurry was to get us ready for sea again. While the navy yard workers were repairing damage, we re-provisioned the ship with food and stores.

* Photo courtesy of U.S. Navy Department -Naval Historical Center

USS Hornet

After leaving the dry-dock, we left Pearl Harbor on the 28th of May and headed west-north-west. Like all of the others in the radio shack, I was feeling excitement and some turbulence in not knowing where we were going, and what we might be getting into. None of us enlisted men had any idea what was in store for us, but it was evident that the officers knew. We did know that we were to rendezvous with the ships of Task Force 16. We also knew that we were behind the task force as we were steaming at about 20 knots to catch up with them. We knew that Task Force 16 had two carriers, the *Enterprise* and the *Hornet*, when they left Pearl Harbor a day ahead of us. The word we got was that the *Yorktown* and Task Force 17 would be joining Task Force 16 as soon as possible.

On 2 June 1942, we rendezvoused with the ships of Task Force 16 and took up our station as part of the Anti-Submarine Warfare (ASW) screen and a plane guard for the *Enterprise*.

Those of us in the enlisted ranks did not get any word from the officers as to what was coming up. On 3 June 1942, we received an urgent message from the Navy base at Dutch Harbor in Alaska reporting that they were under air attack from Japanese carrier planes.

I rushed the message up to the bridge to show the captain and the executive officer. They both looked at this urgent message, yet didn't show any surprise and no concern.

The task force did not change course to head for Alaska but just kept steaming a west-north-west direction.

Across the passageway from the radio shack was the coding room. This room contained the electric coding machine (ECM) used to decipher the coded messages sent from Pearl Harbor 24 hours a day. There was a coding board made up of three commissioned officers that ran the ECM, and they were the only ones allowed to operate the machine. One of these officers finally came into the radio shack, and told us that we were heading for Midway Atoll to repel a Japanese attack and attempted amphibious landing that was scheduled to start the next day, 4 June 1942. Now we understood why the Task Forces had ignored the attack on Dutch Harbor in the morning.

We were feeling excitement, and the anticipation of the action that was to come gave me a feeling of enjoyment. I was really looking forward to what was to happen.

Late in the afternoon of 3 June, we received a message from a PBY Catalina flying search west of Midway. They had spotted a large number of Japanese ships 700 miles west of Midway heading east. These ships were later identified as the Japanese amphibious task group.

* Photo courtesy of U.S. Navy Department -Naval Historical Center

PBY Catalina

Early morning 4 June 1942, we went to GQ an hour before sunrise, and the *Yorktown* began launching several SBD scout planes at about 5:30am. At 05:45am, a PBY Catalina scout plane from Midway reported sighting many Japanese planes headed toward Midway at 150 miles from the Atoll. We secured from GQ at about 6:00 a.m. for breakfast, but at 6:30 we went back to battle stations as the Japanese attack planes arrived over Midway.

The *Enterprise* and the *Hornet* turned into the wind to start launching attack planes for a strike against the Japanese carriers.

Finally by 8:15 a.m., our carriers had launched 155 aircraft for the strike against the Japanese carriers. At 08:20 a.m., a floatplane from one of the Japanese cruisers sighted the *Yorktown*, which had become separated from us by about 12 miles.

This separation occurred because the *Yorktown* had launched and recovered scout planes while TF 16 was heading toward the Japanese carriers.

The U.S. carrier planes were supposed to carry out a coordinated attack in which the dive-bombers would come diving from 10,000 feet and the torpedo planes would come in just over the water. They should have had fighter planes escorting them in during their attack. It took our carriers quite some time to launch 155 planes, so some of the torpedo planes were running low on fuel so they departed toward the last reported position of the Japanese carriers.

The last reported position of the enemy carriers was in error, and with three different air groups from our three carriers, a coordinated attack by 155 planes was more than could be expected. The torpedo planes arrived early without fighter escort. Some of the dive-bombers got lost and had to return to their carriers, and the squadron of bombers from the *Yorktown* sighted a Japanese destroyer going at high speed, so they followed it and sighted the four Japanese carriers.

Our torpedo planes started their attack against the four Japanese carriers at about 10:00 a.m. Most of our TBDs and TBFs were shot down by the Zero fighters. About a half a dozen managed to drop their torpedos, but none scored a hit.

About 10 minutes later, our dive-bombers arrived over the scene and started their attacks. Our SBD dive-bombers caught the Japanese fighters and their carriers by surprise. The Japanese fighters were all down at low altitude attacking our torpedo planes and did not have time to climb up to 10,000 feet and engage our dive-bombers. Also, the Japanese carriers did not have any radar to detect our SBDs so they were able to carry out their attacks without having to fight off the Zeros.

On the *Aylwin*, we were monitoring the pilots radio transmissions and they were reporting bomb hits on three of the large Japanese carriers. Our pilots reported large uncontrolled fires on three of the Japanese carriers. After our experience in the Coral Sea battle, this was sure a welcome report which had us all excited; however, we felt that we would probably still come under attack from the enemy planes, since they now had our position.

The *Yorktown* came under attack by Japanese VAL dive bombers and Kate Torpedo planes at 12:00. We could see the attack as they were now about 10 miles from our position.

We saw a large column of smoke coming from the *Yorktown* as she fought off the attacking planes. The *Yorktown's* F4F fighters were engaged in escorting the torpedo planes and the dive bombers on their strike against the Japanese carriers. The few fighters that were available and the anti-aircraft fire from the ships were not enough to break up the attacking Japanese planes.

* Photo courtesy of U.S. Navy Department -Naval Historical Center

Yorktown Taking a Hit

In less than 1 hour, the smoke disappeared and she was recovering her planes from their strike against the Japanese. The *Yorktown* had lost her radar and radio antennas, so Admiral Fletcher gave up overall command to Admiral Spruance, and Fletcher went aboard a cruiser.

Admiral Spruance on the *Enterprise* took overall command of the U.S. ships and ordered some of the screening ships in the *Enterprise* group to leave and go to the aid of the *Yorktown*. This left the *Enterprise* group with only two cruisers and three destroyers. At 2:30 p.m., the *Yorktown* was attacked again by more Japanese torpedo and dive-bombers. This time the torpedo planes scored 3 hits and the carrier became dead in the water. Captain Buckmeister ordered the *Yorktown* crew to abandon ship. Now, the planes from the *Yorktown* that were still airborne had to land on our other two carriers.

One TBD came back with so much of its wing shot away that it had to land in the water. The *Aylwin* steamed over and picked up the pilot and gunner. Now, we had witnesses of the attack on the Japanese ships.

One hour later, the *Enterprise* and the *Hornet* turned into the wind to launch a strike against the fourth Japanese carrier. Again, the Japanese were caught by surprise as our dive-bombers scored hits on their fourth carrier. The *Enterprise* pilots reported this fourth carrier ablaze from huge explosions with a towering smoke column. As we were to learn later, this signaled the destruction of the fourth large Japanese fleet carrier. We took our position as plane guard for the *Enterprise*, and cheered the returning planes.

On 5 June, our two carriers launched search aircraft and they were able to find two Japanese cruisers which had been damaged and were steaming west very slowly. Our two carriers launched another strike against these ships, and were able to sink one cruiser, but the second one got away after being badly damaged above the water line. In two days of the largest naval battle of all times, we had won a resounding victory.

How were we able to inflict so much damage on them and not suffer any more damage than we did? Task Force 16 was not attacked all day, and we did not fire one round of anti-aircraft fire.

To understand why events turned out as they did, I need to explain four very important topics. The first, was Admiral Yamamoto's grand strategy for a massive attack on the U.S. Pacific fleet and the invasion of Midway Atoll in the central Pacific. Before the attack on Midway, Yamamoto planned to have a two carrier task force conduct an air raid on Dutch Harbor in the Aleutians and invade Kiska and Attu Islands in the end of the Aleutian chain. These attacks were to create a diversion of the U.S. Task Force. When this occurred he planned for one of the main units of the combined fleet to attack Midway with a four-carrier task force. He reasoned that these actions would force the American Pacific fleet to leave Pearl Harbor and come to the aid of Midway. Admiral Yamamoto would be lying in wait with his main battle force that would then close on the unsuspecting American carrier force and annihilate it. Then, his amphibious fleet would invade Midway and give the Japanese an operating base to mount air strikes against Hawaii.

The most crucial requirement of this massive operation was for the Americans to be caught by surprise and react as he predicted. As far as we know, he had no contingency plans on how to operate if the Americans did not react as he wanted.

To detect any movements of the American fleet out of Pearl Harbor, he planned to have a flying boat from Truk Atoll land at French Frigate Shoals in the middle of the Hawaiian chain, and refuel from a submarine. Then, this flying boat would make a scouting sortie over Pearl Harbor and report on how many American warships were in port. The Japanese had conducted such a scouting mission in January 1942 over Pearl Harbor. Yamamoto further ordered a scouting force of Japanese submarines be stationed between Midway and Hawaii to detect and report any early movement of the American task forces toward Midway.

Admiral Nimitz was aware of the January refueling of the EMELY flying boats at French Frigate Shoal, so he ordered the seaplane tender *USS Ballard* to anchor in the bay at the shoal. When the Japanese submarine arrived to wait for the EMELY, it found the bay already occupied, so it had to turn back to Truk Atoll and cancel the scouting mission.

The magnitude of Yamamoto's operation was so complex that the scouting line of Japanese submarines did not all receive their copies of the orders in time to arrive on station, resulting in their being one day late. As a result, our Task Forces 16 and 17 had already passed their location and were at a point well to the west of the Japanese submarine scout line.

As a further step to insure he had timely data on our location, Yamamoto had a scouting plan that involved the float planes from each of the cruisers in his Task Force. Each plane was assigned a pie slice section to patrol and this should have given him timely information on our location before he attacked Midway.

However, the cruiser *Tone's* scout plane was assigned to the sector where we were located, had trouble with a jammed launcher, so their plane was an hour late in being launched, therefore, it did not detect our presence until the Japanese attack on Midway was well under way.

Admiral Nagumo, in charge of the four carriers, was robbed of vital information. He was recovering the initial strike on Midway, and was rearming planes with high explosives bombs for another strike against Midway when the *Tone's* pilot made his late contact report. Therefore, he ordered the arming be changed to armor piercing bombs and torpedos. In their rush to rearm the planes, the Japanese sailors just stacked the bombs taken off to planes on the flight deck and hanger deck.

At that time our planes arrived and started their attack, the Japanese carriers had stacks of high explosive ammunition on deck which had not been returned to their ammunition magazines and the planes on deck were being refueled and were not ready to be launched again. When our bombs hit, they started uncontrolled fires on three of the four carriers. Unfortunately, our torpedo planes started their strike without our F4F fighters and the Japanese ZEROs made quick work of shooting most of them down. On the *Enterprise*, only two TBD torpedo bombers returned, and on the *Hornet*, none of their TBDs returned. One TBD pilot, Ensign Gay, survived and he witnessed the destruction of the Japanese carriers while hanging on to some wreckage. He was picked up by a PBY two days later.

The second topic I need to explain is intelligence operations that were going on in May 1942, both at Pearl Harbor and in Washington D.C. The intelligence officer for the Pacific Fleet was Commander Edwin T. Layton and the officer heading up the cryptographic organization was Lieutenant Commander Joseph J. Rochefort.

This cryptographic group at Pearl Harbor was code named HYPO and in Washington the group was code named NEGAT. Both of these groups were under the Director of Naval Intelligence (OP-20-G). The HYPO unit did not report to the Commander in Chief Pacific Fleet; however, they had been ordered to keep Commander Layton and Admiral Nimitz informed. Both Layton and Rochefort had been naval attaches in Tokyo for several years and both could read and speak Japanese.

Rochefort also became the Navy's top expert in the Japanese Naval radio procedures. Rochefort and his crew at HYPO had been making progress in breaking portions of the Japanese Naval operating code (JN25A). They had not broken many single messages completely, but had broken parts of a large number of coded messages. By making comparison of portions of various messages that could be read, Rochefort was able to obtain valuable information.

Rochefort knew that the Japanese Navy intended to switch to a new code on 1 May 1942, but they experienced problems getting new code books to all of the ships in their Navy. Therefore, Rochefort was able to keep reading portions of their messages until about 26 May when they switched to their new code JN25B. Breaking the new code would take several weeks of working on it before he could start getting information from it. The U.S. Navy was most fortunate that the Japanese delayed switching to the new code, for this gave Rochefort and his crew a chance to obtain extremely valuable information on Yamamoto's operations.

At NEGAT, the Director of Naval Communications was Captain Joseph R. Redman and his brother Commander John R. Redman was head of a Combat Intelligence Unit in Washington.

This was on the same level that Rochefort held in HYPO. HYPO and NEGAT units shared information available at either station. Since both were working from the same information from the crytographers, they both should have come to the same intelligence predictions of enemy intentions. In analyzing the point of attack refered to as point AF, Rochefort and Layton predicted that the most probable point of attack by the Japanese combined fleet was Midway Atoll.

The Redmans in Washington predicted that the Japanese would attack in the Southwest Pacific. They were not as adept in the analysis as Layton and Rochefort, but the Redmans had the ear of the Commander in Chief of the U.S. Navy, Admiral King in Washington. Admiral King told Admiral Nimitz that he should maintain a task force in the Southwest Pacific to counter any Japanese thrust further southward in that area.

Admiral Nimitz was convinced that Layton and Rochefort were correct in their analysis of the Japanese fleet movements. Therefore, he ordered Admiral Halsey to make a showing of his Task Force 16 to the Japanese in the southwest Pacific area and then head straight to Pearl Harbor to join Admiral Fletcher and Task Force 17. The problem facing Nimitz was how to convince Admiral King in Washington that his staff in Hawaii had the correct analysis that Midway Atoll was the target of the Japanese attacks.

Fortunately, the Navy still had the underwater cable from Pearl Harbor to Midway. Layton and Rochefort proposed that a message be sent over this submarine cable to Midway ordering them to come up on a radio channel in plain language, stating that the water evaporation plant in Midway had broken down and they were in urgent need of fresh water.

The only source of fresh water at Midway was the evaporation of sea water. Admiral Nimitz approved the ruse and the message was sent.

The Japanese took the bait and one of their monitoring stations reported to Truk Atoll by radio, that AF had reported it was in urgent need of fresh water. This proved that the point of the Japanese attack was Midway Atoll, and Admiral King notified Admiral Nimitz that he should go ahead with his plan for defending Midway.

The Combat Intelligence Unit at HYPO still did not have a date and time of the attack. The date-time group in all dispatches was in super encipher code they had not been able to break. Finally, on 24 May, two of the cryptographers at HYPO managed to decipher this group, and Admiral Nimitz now knew where and when to expect the Japanese attack. The two-carrier task force would strike Kodiak and Dutch Harbor on 3 June 1942, and the four carrier force would strike Midway on 4 June.

The intelligence summary of 26 May also told Nimitz that they would hit Midway from the northwest at a distance of 175 miles, and it gave the approximate time of launching of attack aircraft. When the battle was over, Nimitz called a meeting of his entire staff in which he told them that Layton and Rochefort were only off by 5 miles in range, 5 degrees in bearing and 5 minutes in time in their predicted launching point of the Japanese attack.

Therefore, the requirement of Yamamoto's operation plan that the U.S. Navy be caught by surprise was breached. Also, his plan for his scouting forces that were to keep him informed about our movements was a bust as described above.

Another factor leading to the defeat of the Japanese was their lack of air search radar. When our torpedo planes arrived early, all of their ZERO fighters were engaged in the destruction of our TBDs at low altitude and no one detected our SBD dive bombers coming in a high altitude.

Finally, the last factor that accounted for the Japanese defeat was the fact that Yamamoto's operation plan called for his forces to be widely separated over some 1000 square miles.

His main battle line of battleships, cruisers and destroyers were separated from the Fast Carrier Fleet by some 300 miles, so he could not get concentrated antiaircraft fire when we struck their carriers. He also had a fleet with two of his carriers conducting a strike against Alaska, which was ineffectual in that it did not cause the U.S. Navy to rush up to Alaska. His Amphibious Fleet was some 400 miles southwest of his carriers, so they could offer no support when we attacked.

Unlike the U.S. Navy, the Japanese did not make an attempt to make urgent repairs to the *Shokaku* and the *Zuikaku* after the Coral Sea Battle. If the Japanese had made urgent repairs as we did to the *Yorktown*, and these two carriers had been at Midway, the outcome might have been quite different. So, the damage that we made to those two carriers at Coral Sea was very significant on the results at Midway.

All of these factors going against the Japanese can only be

explained by knowing that God was on our side, and he was looking out for us.

Even though we were not under attack during the action, it was still an exciting time monitoring the radio traffic from our attacking planes, and seeing the action going on around the *Yorktown*.

She did not go down until the following day when a Japanese submarine torpedoed her. The crew had extinguished the fires, and preparations were being made to take her under tow back to Pearl Harbor when the Japanese sub found her. When the Japanese submarine found the *Yorktown*, the destroyer *Hammonn* was tied up alongside the Y*orktown*, furnishing electrical power and fire fighting water and hoses. One of the torpedos struck the *Hammonn* first and she broke in two and sank in just a few minutes. Some of the six hundred pound depth charges had not been set on safe and all of the depth charges exploded as the stern sank.

This explosion along with the other torpedos ended up sinking the *Yorktown*.

The Battle of Midway has been judged by most experts as the most decisive battle in the U.S.

history. The losses for both sides are given below:

	Japan	*U.S.*
Causalities	2,500	307
Carriers	4	1
Cruisers	1	0
Destroyers	0	1
Aircraft	332	147

Next to the loss of 4 fleet carriers, the loss of one Japanese Zero fighter in the Aleutians probably runs a close second to the loss of so many experienced pilots and senior commissioned officers. This aircraft was recovered in the Aleutians and shipped to San Diego where it underwent extensive flight tests, which identified the weakness of certain characteristics. These points were taken into consideration in the design changes in the Navy's new F6F Hellcat fighter to give our fighters an edge over the Zero.

• Of the 6,477 Japanese aircraft destroyed in WWII, 4,947 were demolished by Hellcats
• The Japanese were not able to operate offensively again after 6 June 1942.
• This battle marked the beginning of the U.S. offensive operations leading to victory in the
Pacific in 1945

In 1997, The Secretary of the Navy turned over the custodianship of Midway Island to The Department of Interior's Fish and Wildlife Service, and the "Gooney" birds have reclaimed their home. These birds are actually Laysan albatross, and there is now an estimated 800,000 birds nesting on Eastern Island. With the inclusion of jet aircraft in the Navy, the air strips on Eastern Island were closed and new longer air strips were built on Sand Island. There are now so many birds on Midway Atoll that aircraft can only land and take off at night. In 1998, Robert D. Ballard (discoverer of the *Titanic*) returned to Midway with his crew and deep submergence robot, to search for the *Yorktown*. They found her and made a number of photographs as she lies more than 17,000 feet deep in the waters off of Midway.

6

First Aleutian Duty

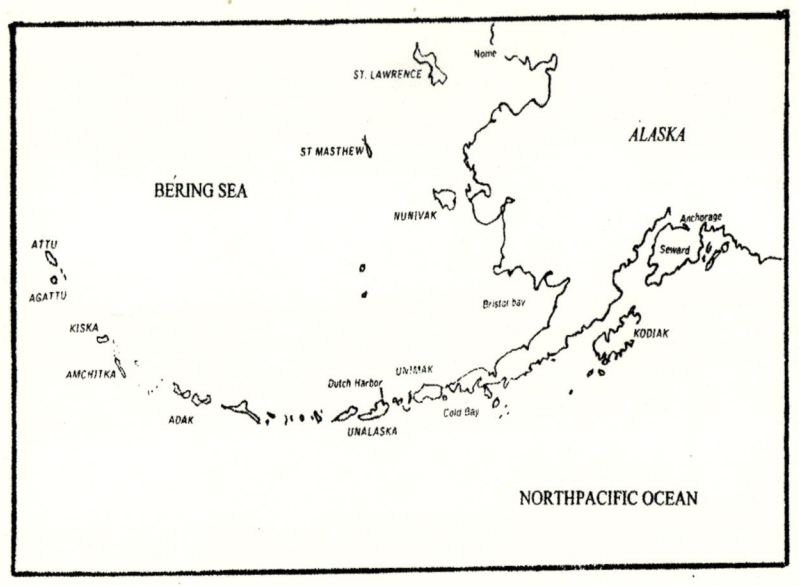

ALEUTIAN ISLANDS

At the conclusion of the Battle of Midway, on 11 June 1942, we were returning with Task Force 16 to Pearl Harbor when we were detached from TF16. We were ordered to escort the tanker *Kaskaskia* (AO27) to Alaska, where we joined Task Force 8 in the Aleutians on 14 June.

This was an uneventful trip with good weather and smooth sailing. TF8 had originally been ordered to intercept the Japanese raid on Dutch Harbor. However, the Admiral in charge did not believe the estimates of Rochefort and Layton on the position from which the Japanese would launch their attack, so he made his own estimate, which was completely wrong. TF8 did not get near the Japanese Task Force conducting the strike on Dutch Harbor. After the raid on Dutch Harbor, the Japanese made amphibious landings on Kiska and Attu Islands at the western end of the Aleutian chain.

This was a great embarrassment to the U.S. Navy in that the Japanese landings were unopposed. Our intelligence estimates knew of the raid on Dutch Harbor but did not have any details on the proposed landings on Kiska and Attu Islands. Task Force 8 was ordered to scout out the situation in the Aleutians so those plans could be made for our amphibious attacks to take these islands back under U.S. control.

Nothing very exciting happened as we spent most of our time patrolling along the Aleutian chain, and being summer, the weather was good and the days were long. The sun would come up about 3:00 a.m. and set about 10:30 p.m. Some of the days the islands were fog bound so we couldn't see much. On the days that the fog lifted, we got to see some of the beautiful islands with their snow-capped mountains. We would stop at Kodiak Island, where the Navy had established an operating base where we would get supplies, spare parts and needed fuel.

On one end of our patrol we would sail close to Kiska, which was engulfed in fog, and bombard the island with our five-inch guns. This was just routine shelling, and the Japanese never returned our fire. I was no longer involved with the five-inch gun mounts as I was standing watches in the radio shack and on the radar control console. This duty tended to be a little boring due to very little action.

The most interesting thing that happened while we were on patrol, occurred one day when the gyrocompass failed and the navigator had to switch to the magnetic compass. Since we were so far north and were traveling east and west on patrol, the variations in the magnetic compass were substantial, and they had to make corrections in the ships heading several times a day. There was a lot of pressure from the captain and the exec officer to get the gyrocompass fixed.

The gyrocompass has electrical circuits that operate repeaters on the bridge and in the pilothouse. It is usually the job of the chief electrician to maintain this system. However, our chief electrician did not really know how a gyroscope worked.

Part of the main battery gun control system had a gyroscope, which was used to keep the guns on a correct angle of elevation from the actual horizon when the ship rolled. The exec is the navigator on a destroyer, and he asked the chief fire-controlman to take a look. The chief firecontrolman then asked me to join him in fixing the gyrocompass, since I had studied gyros in my first physics course at the University of Kansas. It took us a while, but we finally found the problem and got the gyrocompass running again. We told the exec that the chief electrician had fixed it and that made everybody happy.

The *Aylwin* left TF8 on 10 July 1942, to escort the *Kaskaskia* back to Pearl Harbor, arriving there on 17 July. From that date until 31 July, the ship was in the Navy Yard at Pearl Harbor undergoing repairs. This layover gave us an opportunity to get liberty and travel around the island of Oahu. Some of my buddies from the radio shack got a hotel room in Honolulu where they had a stock of liquor. I didn't spend any time there, because I really wasn't a drinking sailor.

During our stay at Pearl Harbor, the Navy Yard installed a model SG surface search radar and a model FD fire control radar. These radars had a much narrower beam than the SC-1 air search radar, and they had a much more accurate range measuring unit. The SG system made it possible to keep station on the fleet guide at night without having to guess at the range to the guide. I spent most of my time aboard watching the installation of these systems.

The operating controls for the FD fire control system were located in the main battery gun director that was on the deck above the bridge deck. This director controlled the five-inch guns and it contained the mechanical computer, as well as the optical equipment. This was the only class destroyer that had the electromechanical computer up in the director. The director was not enclosed with a blast shield. The director on the *Aylwin* was open from the waist up, but it did have a convertible top like the tops of convertible cars. My new battle station was operating the range unit on the FD radar system in the director. Being in the director gave us as great view of any action that was going on during general quarters. It was the best place on the ship to see what was happening as we had unobstructed view in all directions.

7

Guadalcanal

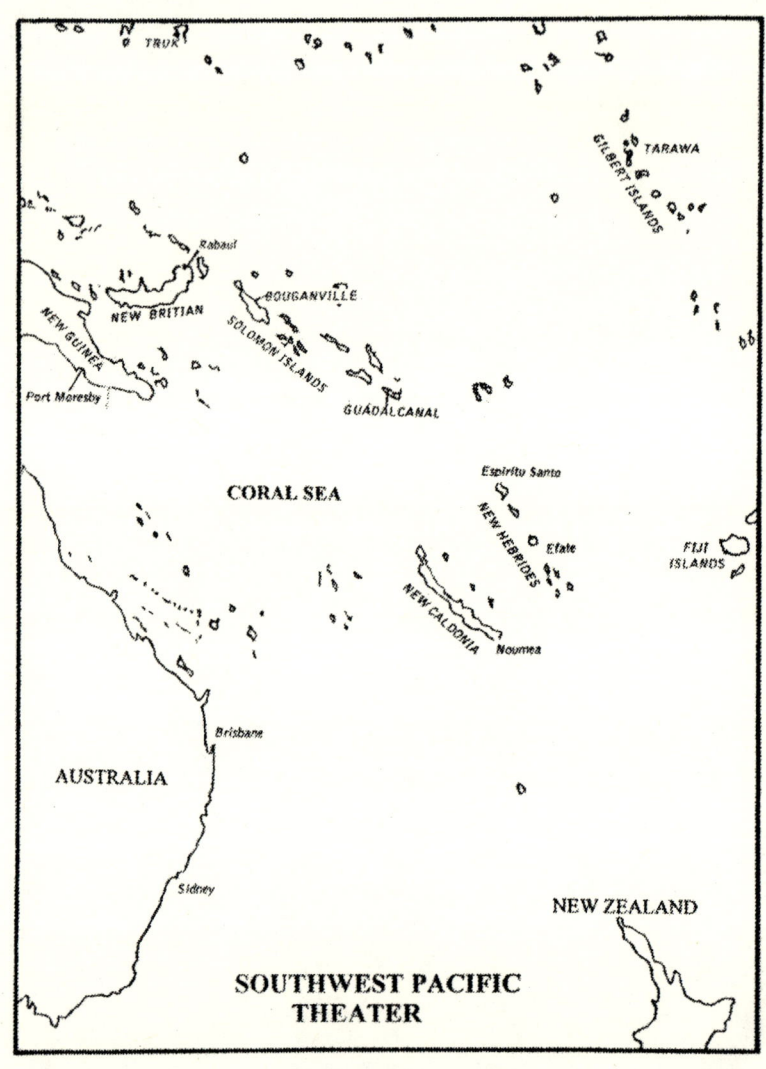

*Guadalcanal is an island located in the southern
end of the Solomon chain*

The *Aylwin* left Pearl Harbor on 2 August 1942, to escort the *Long Island* (AVG1), which was carrying a marine fighter squadron headed for Guadalcanal. The *Long Island* was converted from a merchant ship to an auxiliary aircraft carrier.

They could not carry on regular air operations, but could launch planes when the carrier arrived at the destination. Our Marines had landed on Guadalcanal and they needed this fighter squadron for ground support, and for intercepting Japanese air raids from Rabul.

* Photo courtesy of U.S. Navy Department -Naval Historical Center

Long Island CVE-1

The trip down from Pearl Harbor was uneventful, except for crossing the equator again. This time, I was one of the guys with a paddle at the end of the canvas tube. It was all in fun and it sure broke up the monotony of steady sailing with no aircraft activities.

The U.S. Marines had landed at Guadalcanal and taken over the airfield that the Japanese had built. This airstrip was called *Henderson Field*, named after Major Lofton Henderson UCMC who died while leading a squadron of dive-bombers in the Battle of Midway.

I was getting used to the routine of living aboard. My bunk was now in the after petty officers PO compartment. A typical compartment is shown below, although this picture was not taken on the *Aylwin*.

* Photo courtesy of the United States Naval Institute

Crew Sleeping Compartment

When I first moved to the (PO) compartment, I was assigned to the bottom bunk in a stack of bunks four high. At first, I thought that this was going to be just great. However, when the first General Quarters Klaxton alarm went off while we were sleeping, I rolled over and ended up on my hands and knees on the deck. Before I could stand up, a pair of feet landed on the middle of my back when the fellow in the top bunk came down. Then, the fellow in number 2 bunk landed on my back. Shortly after, number 3 did the same. By this time, my back was beginning to hurt, and I decided that in the future I would stay put until the three top fellows were clear.

After a couple of months, I got moved to a bunk on the starboard side bulkhead where the bunks were only three high, and we all had lockers under the bottom bunk. The mattresses were all made with horsehair and about an inch and a half thick.

We were issued a sheet that was made like a pillowcase that covered the mattress. We were also given a blanket and pillow. We had two straps with metal hooks on each end that were put across the mattress and the hooks were secured to the pipe frame of the bunk. When the straps were secured, we could then fold the bunk up against the bulkhead for the day.

One night, we were experiencing rough weather and the ship was rolling so far from side to side that I was having a rough time staying in the bunk. I took the bunk straps, and secured myself in the bunk, and just as I was going to sleep, the GQ alarm went off. In my hurry to get out, I found that I was having trouble getting the straps off. It took me so much time that I got dogged down in the compartment and never did get to my battle station. The Petty Officer's compartment was a deck below the main deck, and when we were going to battle stations, there was a watertight cover over the ladder going down into the PO compartment. It had about a dozen dogs around the outer edges of the cover to secure it and make sure it was tight against the rubber gasket, thereby making it water tight. So there was no way for me to get out after they closed the cover. Needless to say, I never did that again.

About once a week, the word would be passed to air bedding. I would go below, get my mattress, blanket, and bunk straps, and take them all topside to the main deck. There, we would hang them over the lifelines and secure them with the bunk straps. After about four hours, the word was passed to take all bedding below. Airing of bedding was only done during routine sailing.

The entire inside of the washroom and toilets was stainless steel. This made the washroom easy to clean up and kept it looking good.

Fresh water on a Navy ship was always a precious commodity because it had to be distilled from the seawater, and the boilers always had first call on fresh water. There was a laundry on board, but it was very small and it was used mainly for washing the clothes of the officers and the chief petty officers. Most of the rest of us in the crew washed our clothes by hand.

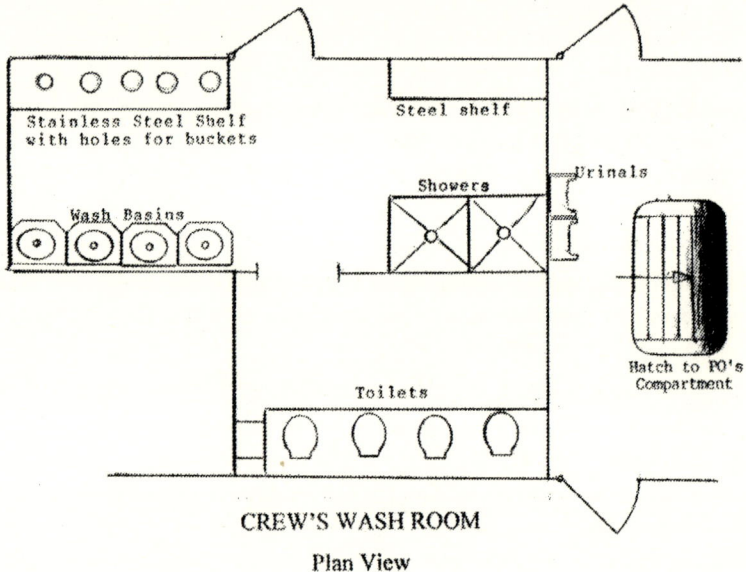

CREW'S WASH ROOM

Plan View

To wash clothes, shave and take a shower, I would get a bucket of fresh hot water and pour some into the wash basin for shaving.

After shaving, soap powder was added to the bucket and the bucket was placed in one of the holes shown in the picture, and I scrubbed my clothes. After washing the clothes, the rest of the soapy water was used to clean our bodies. After soaping up, I would then get into the shower to rinse off. We would only be allowed to turn the shower water on long enough to rinse off the soap. This procedure insured that the crew used only a minimum of fresh water each day.

The two evaporators that were used to distill the seawater were located in the engine room. When they would get clogged up with salt deposits, the engineers would shut one down for cleaning. Since the steam plant had first call on fresh water, when an evaporator was being cleaned we would have to wash off using seawater.

We had to wear white hats at all times, so when we washed our hats we would add liquid chlorine bleach and let them soak for a while. One day, one of the fellows got some powdered bleach and we decided to give it a try. We left the hats soaking in a bucket for about four hours and when we tried to lift them out of the bucket they came out in chunks of cloth. The bleach had eaten away all of the stitching. So much for powdered bleach.

On the sides of both smokestacks at the main deck level were large exhaust blowers that drained the hot air from the three boiler rooms. In front of these blowers we would string up short lines and hang our clothes to dry. While in the tropics, the clothes would dry in a half an hour in front of the hot air from the fire rooms. To mend clothing, I would have to sew most things by hand. The signalmen did have a portable sewing machine that they would let us use from time to time. The pants of our dress blues had a flap on the front with 13 buttons to secure it.

The buttons were attached by machine, and there was a thread sticking out of the center of each button. If this thread got caught on anything and it pulled this thread, the button would come off. Whenever I got a new pair of pants, I had to remove all 13 buttons and sew them all back by hand so that they would not come off by accident.

Before we left Pearl Harbor, we picked up some new recruits. One of these fellows was a rough character from the Chicago inner city area. He didn't believe in bathing every day. When his odor got so bad that we couldn't take it any more, we took him back to the wash room, stripped off his clothes and scrubbed him down with stiff bristled scrub brushes until his skin turned red.

We took his clothes, tied them to one end of a line and threw them over the stern of the ship with the other end of the line tied to a cleat on the deck. He got the word, and we never had to clean him up again.

Also among the new crewmembers was a young fellow who didn't seem very well adjusted to life aboard a fighting ship. One evening, he climbed up on one of the 600 pound depth charge racks on the fantail, and jumped overboard. I couldn't figure what he was trying to do, as we were several hundred miles from the nearest land. The ship was turned around and he was picked up, and from that time on until we got into port he was watched at all times.

The radioman that I stood watch with, Ulrich, was also the unofficial ship's barber. Since there was no place for a barbershop on board a destroyer, he would set up to cut hair on the fantail. There he would turn an empty garbage can upside down and the victim would sit on the can and he would go to work. He did such a good job that even the captain and the exec would have him come up to the wardroom and cut their hair.

When we were not too far from land, and there was no activity going on, we liked to look out over the water and pick out albatross skimming just over the surface of the water looking for fish. They were amazing birds who hardly used any energy flying across the water. They would get as low to the surface of the water as they could without going in, and utilize the small updraft caused by the water evaporating to give them lift on their wings. They could glide this way for several hundred yards, and then they would suddenly lift off and circle around and then go in another direction.

The albatross have wingspans of over six feet and they have a joint about a third of the way in from the tip. As they would sail along just over the surface of the water, a small wave near their tip would come up, they could lift just the third of that wing until the water receded and then let it back down again. Watching them was such a peaceful and relaxing experience that it was hard to remember that we were at war.

The crew's mess hall was located one deck below the main deck under the officer's wardroom. Just forward of the galley was the start of the fo'c'sle and the wardroom was under the fo'c'sle deck. In the mess hall, there were steam tables on the port side of the mess hall and the rest of the space was taken up with tables and benches secured to the deck. The food was generally good, depending on what the cooks had to work with.

When the stock of food was getting low, some of the meals were pretty bad. When we were in the southwest Pacific, sometimes our choice of meat for dinner would be ram, lamb, mutton or sheep. Of course, these were supplied from New Zealand. I can remember a few times when we ran so low on food that our dinner was what we called "shit on a shingle," better know to you as chipped beef on toast. Our cooks were great guys, and they did everything they could to make our meals as good as possible.

Every evening after dinner, those of us not on watch would go to the galley to get coffee and go aft to the fantail and listen to music. In the galley there were two large steam-heated vats that held about 30 to 40 gallons of liquid. The cook would fill the vat with water and take a sack about the size of a small pillow and fill it with coffee grounds and immerse it in the steaming water. I felt that this made pretty strong coffee, but the cook would lift the sack up and push in the side with a ladle and fill his cup with that thick juice. This vat of coffee was left on low steam heat for the rest of the night to supply the fellows on night watch. Needless to say, by the 4 to 8 watch in the morning, this coffee tasted pretty rotten. That is why we had our own coffeepot in the radio shack.

One afternoon, I got a call from the Chief Fire controlman, Worrell. He was having trouble with the training mechanism on one of the gun mounts and he needed some help. The training mechanism turns the gun mount around in the horizontal plane. He knew that I had training on the mechanism that turned the radar antennas, so he called on me. We had quite a time, but finally got it fixed. From that time on, when there was any kind of electrical control problem or electrical-mechanical problem, they would call Worrell and me to take a look.

The period after dinner was one that we all looked forward to each day, because we could go aft, listen to music, visit, and wait for sunset when we all had to go to general quarters. Even the officers would come aft on the gun deck (one deck above the main deck), and look down on us having a good time, enjoying the music.

While we were underway during this period the task force did not have any carriers left; the *Wasp* had been sunk at Guadalcanal, The *Saratoga* was in the Navy Yard in Bremerton, Washington, and the *Enterprise* was at Pearl harbor undergoing repairs.

We were steaming in the South West Pacific without air cover, and morale was at a low ebb. The general feeling of those of us in the crew was that it was just a matter of time before we too would be sunk, as so many of our tin cans had done.

Every night in the Chief's quarters, there was a big poker game in which hundreds of dollars would change hands. Nobody seemed to care if he lost so much money, because they felt that we could be sunk at any time.

On August 13, 1942, we arrived at Suva Fiji, where we entered the harbor and anchored for a couple of days. This gave us time to relax and enjoy the warm weather.

In this tropical climate, sleeping in our bunks below deck was difficult since we had no air conditioning. Therefore, we would sleep on the open decks. I found that lying on the steel deck was a little uncomfortable at first, but I soon got accustomed to sleeping on my back. I would use my kapok-filled life jacket as a pillow. Of course, I was not the only one sleeping topside. The topside decks were covered with sailors sleeping. Whenever we would sleep on deck, we had to inform boatswain mate where we would be, so he could wake us when we had to go on watch.

One afternoon we got a chance to go ashore and look around. There was not much to buy at any of the little stores, but we did buy some palm fiber mats which we used to sleep on deck. The town was hot and humid and the only interesting thing we saw were some native men playing a table game that looked like dominos. There were a few buildings that were all open, and the place seemed pretty dirty compared to the clean conditions on the ship.

One afternoon, I stepped out on deck and looked up at the bridge where all I could see were binoculars and long glasses looking out toward the island.

I ran up to the bridge to see what was going on and I found the signalmen and quartermasters saying, "Boy, look at that, wow, isn't that something." I finally found another pair of binoculars and looked out where they were watching to see a whole native family taking a bath in a large tub out in the open in amongst the palm trees.

We had been underway for some time with no liberty and some of the fellows who had liberty found a bar, and proceeded to swizzle up on the local ale which was made in Australia. This ale is quite a bit stronger than the U.S. beer and these fellows managed to get high as a kite. They got so tanked up that they couldn't walk when it was time to come back to the ship. They were brought back on a flatbed truck with Fijian policemen. These policemen were Micronesian, and were all very big and strong.

Their uniforms were a throwback to the British in that they had bright red tunics with crossed white belts over their shoulders secured to white waist belts, and cut-off bright blue trousers. They wore no shoes and after the truck stopped each policeman stepped up and grabbed a sailor under each arm and brought them down the dock and aboard.

This was such a comical sight that those of us aboard almost died laughing. It was a real loss in that we had no cameras aboard to record this event.

We got underway the next day, and on August 17th we arrived at Efate, a French controlled island south of the Solomon Islands about 500 miles west of Fiji Island. Efate is a volcanic island of about 350 square miles with a summit of about 2,200 feet. It had rough terrain covered by a rain forest with tropical moist air. At this time France was occupied by the Nazis and she was not able to govern any of her islands, so the British Royal Navy took over control of Efate.

This was to be one of our forward bases for jumping off to Guadalcanal in the Solomon chain where our Marines had landed on August 2, 1942. At Efate we joined up with the *USS Helena, CL-50* and *the USS Dale, DD353*, and left Efate the next day to escort the *Long Island* to Guadalcanal.

As our group neared Guadalcanal on August 20th we heard radio warnings from Australian coast watchers in Japanese held islands further north up the Solomon chain. They were reporting that the Japanese had an air raid coming south from Rabaul toward Guadalcanal. The *Long Island* turned into the wind, picked up speed and started to launch planes. She launched 19 F4F fighters and 12 SBD scout planes. I ran up to the radio shack and we tuned in the plane radio channel. Even before the pilots had a chance to land they had to fight off the air raid on *Henderson* field. It was exciting to hear the exchange between fighter planes and the air controllers on the ground.

With the planes delivered to Guadalcanal our group's mission was completed, so we turned south and returned to Efate Island. We arrived on August 22nd.

When we entered the harbor, there was only a small opening between two other ships alongside the fueling dock. Our captain maneuvered the bow of the ship into the opening, and got lines and hoses over to the dock and we started refueling. A short time later, we saw a British navy officer coming down the dock. He made quite a picture for us to see. All of our navy officers were wearing khaki with small fore and aft campaign hats. This British officer had on a short sleeved white shirt with shoulder boards of a commander. He had on white shorts and white stockings to just below the knees. He was wearing a frame hat with scrambled eggs on the bill. On his upper lip was a large handle bar mustache.

He had on horned rim glasses and was smoking a large pipe. To those of us on the *Aylwin*, he looked so odd that he appeared almost funny to us. When he got to our spot on the dock he stopped, looked up to our bridge and addressed our captain. "I say, old boy, beastly sorry we had to stick you in this bloody old hole." With that we turned our heads and broke out laughing. It was so unreal it struck us as funny. Even now, over 56 years later, I can still see him on that dock and picturing him still brings a smile to my face. After refueling we tied up alongside of a British destroyer at another dock. The first afternoon the British tin can passed the word for everyone to knock off work and lay back to the fantail for tea and crumpets. When our skipper heard about this, he decided that we had to answer in kind. The next afternoon the word was passed on the *Aylwin* to knock off work and lay back to the fantail for coffee and cookies.

We got underway on August 24th. From that date until August 30th we were on antisubmarine patrol off of the harbor's entrance.

One afternoon, we were relieved from patrol to come into the harbor and refuel. We tied up alongside another destroyer. After we had finished refueling, we noticed one of their sailors was sitting alone off to one side so we called him over to talk. When he drew near, I could see that he was still just a kid. I asked him how old he was and he started crying and told me he was only 15. He had lied about his age, and now here he was on a front line destroyer that had been making patrol runs up the Slot in the Solomon Islands almost every night to intercept Japanese convoys supplying their troops on Guadalcanal. He was as scared as anyone I had ever seen. One of the chiefs on their ship told us that their executive officer was having him transferred back to the states.

All of the ships in port still had to copy the broadcast messages from radio station NPM at Pearl Harbor. Our first class radioman, Olsen, would always make an agreement with other ships that only one ship needed to copy NPM, and make duplicates of the messages for the other ships. The ships in the agreement would take turns copying NPM. This gave us a break for a few days by not having to stand continuous radio watches. Since I didn't have to stand radio watches all of the time, it gave me a chance to do maintenance on the radio, radar and sonar equipment.

On the morning of the 30th, we left the dock in Efate and got underway to escort the *Long Island* to Espiritu Santo. Referring to the maps at the beginning of this chapter, Espiritu Santo is the westernmost island of the New Hebrides Group. This group of islands was also a French colony before the WWII. We dropped the *Long Island* off at Espiritu Santo proceeded to Pago Pago in the Samoa group where we arrived on September 5, 1942. We entered the harbor, refueled and tied up for the night.

Early the next morning we got underway, and joined the *Raleigh*,

CL-7 and the *Conyngham, DD371*, in order to escort the *Wharton, AP7* to Canton Island.

The *Wharton* was an attack transport to carry our Marines for amphibious landings. We arrived at Canton on September 11, and screened the *Wharton* from submarines during landing operations. It was interesting watching the landings take place. The *Wharton* got as close to the beach as she could and anchored. She then put landing boats in the water, and the Marines climbed over the sides and down the side netting and into the small landing boats. The boats then carried them to shore. This was a procedure we were to see many times in the future.

On September 18th, the *Aylwin* was directed to join the *USS North Carolina BB5*, which had been torpedoed, and escort her back to Pearl Harbor for repairs. The trip back to Pearl was routine, and we enjoyed the smooth sailing in safe waters. Again, I have to mention the beautiful sunsets that we enjoyed each evening while at General Quarters. It was hard to believe sometimes that we were at war, because the surrounding water and sky were so peaceful.

We arrived back at Pearl Harbor on September 30, 1942, and went alongside the *USS Dixie AD14*, a destroyer tender, for repairs and maintenance. The *Aylwin* spent the month of October 1942 at Pearl Harbor undergoing maintenance and conducting training exercises with various cruisers and battle ships offshore from Oahu.

October 4th, I received orders to report to the Pacific Fleet Radar School at Pearl Harbor. I packed up all of my belongings in a sea bag, and reported to the school where I was assigned to a barracks building second floor for sleeping quarters. The bunks were two-tiered, but there were only 16 of us so we all had bottom bunks. Outside, the mosquitoes were thick, and I seemed to be just the bait they were looking for. I ended up with quite a number of bites.

At least the barracks building had screens on the windows so we were able to sleep well at night. About the third night when we went to bed, we noticed that all of the screens had been removed.

That night we were assaulted by swarms of the little critters. I would hear someone holler, "Here come the dive bombers I'm hit, help." This went on all night. The next day, I found the third class boatswain who was in charge of the barracks and registered our complaints. It turned out he was an old time sailor and didn't like radiomen — he called us radio girls.

He claimed that he had sent the screens to be repaired and they were lost. So we took matters in our own hands and went to Marine Small Stores, got mosquito netting, tied it to the bottom of the top bunk, thereby making an enclosure where we could get some relief.

Being stationed on land at the school sure was a welcome change after a year at sea. I enjoyed eating in the mess hall and getting to see a movie in the evening once in a while. Of course, we had Sundays off, which gave us a chance to travel around the island and see some of the sights. Most evenings we sat around and exchanged our experiences during the first year of the war at sea. In other words we told sea stories, and some were real whoppers.

School was challenging, but interesting, and it was good to get to talk to other technicians who had all experienced some of the unique problems we encountered and had managed to correct them. When I completed the course, the *Aylwin* had already left Pearl Harbor and was proceeding to the Navy Yard at Mare Island, California.

8

Mare Island

Since the *Aylwin* had already left for San Francisco by the time I finished the Pacific Fleet Radar School, I was assigned to the *USS Barker DD213*, an old WW I destroyer, for transportation to San Francisco. After we got underway from Pearl Harbor, I was put to work with the deck gang chipping paint. This was not hard work, but it was boring. As the chipping got deeper into old paint, the chief boatswain came by and said, "Don't chip so deep, the paint is the only thing holding this old bucket together." The chow was not anything to write home about, but it was good enough to get by for the six days it would take to get to San Francisco.

I found the radio shack, and volunteered to stand watches on the radio station NPM broadcast from Pearl Harbor. The radio shack was smaller than the one on the *Aylwin*, having only two operating positions, but it was good to get out of the deck gang. The chief radioman was really good. He would come in to the radio shack when the press wireless news broadcast was scheduled to start. He would get a cup of coffee, sit down at one of the operating positions, take out a blank sheet of paper and feed into the typewriter while the Morse code was coming in at 32 words per minute. He would finally start typing and catch up with the code, but he would stay two to three words behind it all of the time. I had tried copying press wireless, but made too many mistakes. I just needed more practice to get readable copy.

Their method of making coffee was as old as the ship. They had a hot plate in the radio shack and they would put water into a saucepan, put it on the burner, bring it to a boil and then spoon in coffee grounds. Drinking it made our hair stand on end, but we had no trouble staying awake on night watches.

The trip to San Francisco was smooth sailing and that made it a pleasant trip. On December 23rd, we arrived off of San Francisco and I went out on deck to see the sights.

I had never been to San Francisco before. When we started heading under the Golden Gate, I don't think I had ever seen such a beautiful sight. It was a clear day and I could see almost the whole Bay Area. Straight ahead were the Berkeley hills and off to the right were all of the buildings in San Francisco. Seeing all of the homes nestled in the East Bay hills with the blue sky above was such a beautiful scene it took my breath away. After all of the action we had been through, I felt like I was being transported into Paradise. When we were in the South Pacific, I often felt I would never see the United States again, yet here was one of its most beautiful sights.

After passing under the Golden Gate Bridge we turned left and headed for Mare Island arriving there about an hour later. It was good to get back to the *Aylwin* again, but she had been in the Navy Yard for about a week and everything was in a mess. The yard workers had air hoses and electrical lines strung all over the decks, and they were busy with chipping hammers and arc welders all over the ship. The showers on board were not working, so I had to take a shower on the dock. The showers on the dock were not heated; as a matter of fact, they were open to the air at the top of the walls on two sides. Boy, it sure was cold taking a bath in the early morning. December 24th was spent going over the radar work being done while I was away.

On Christmas day, I caught a bus to San Francisco to see this beautiful city. I got off the bus in downtown on Market Street and started walking and looking at all of the tall buildings.

After walking a few blocks, I saw a USO room in one of the buildings on the ground floor facing Market Street. The room was open and there were people inside, so I decided to go in and see what they had to offer. As soon as I stepped in the door, a lady behind a table called to me and wanted to know if I wanted to go to a home for Christmas dinner. Of course I said yes and she gave directions.

I finally arrived at an apartment building and rang the bell. When the door opened, there stood a beautiful blue-eyed blonde, about my age. Her name was Virginia McNamara and she invited me in. We went to an apartment that she shared with her mother and her sister. She had two older brothers, one was in the Navy aboard a PT boat tender in the Pacific, and the other was flying B-26s in Europe. Her sister was married to a doctor who was in the Army in Hawaii.

We hit it off wonderfully and, after a delicious turkey dinner with all of the trimmings, we did the dishes while we talked, and then took her dog out for a walk. I was getting very interested so we made a date for the following Saturday night for dinner. That Saturday I took her to the Palace Hotel, on Market Street, one of San Francisco's best. We had a great steak dinner, but it was getting hard to carry on a conversation with so many people stopping by the table to offer drinks and pat me on the back. Apparently, they had not had a chance to see many sailors who had seen any action in the Pacific. We finished dinner and I took her home to her apartment.

A couple days after that, we went to the Top of the Mark to have a drink and look over the city in the early evening. It was a beautiful sight. I will never forget the times we had together in San Francisco. I promised to write her after we left Mare Island to go to sea again. I began a routine of writing her every day and she did the same. It was great getting a pile of letters every time we got a mail delivery.

9

Aleutians Retaken

While we were still in the Navy Yard at Mare Island on January 7,1943, in accordance with orders, LCDR Malpass relieved CDR Phelan as Commanding Officer of the *Aylwin*. The members of the crew respected CDR Phelan and had grown to like him very much.

This move did not make us in the crew happy. During air attacks, when CDR Phelan was on the bridge, he had a 50-caliber machine gun that he would point up at the attacking planes and fire away. Of course, we all knew that he didn't have a chance of hitting any of the planes as the range of his machine gun was way too short, but we liked his fighting spirit. We had all grown to admire and like CDR Phelan and we hated to see him go. LCDR Malpass had been our Executive Officer since I joined the ship, and we had found him to be all business and not the least bit friendly. As a matter of fact, he could be downright mean at times and always appeared to be very unhappy. The next morning, the *Aylwin* got underway for Dutch Harbor, Unalaska in accordance with orders from Commander Task Force 8. We were steaming alone and were not to join up with another ship until we arrived at Dutch Harbor.

This was January and the weather was kicking up storms, making the riding pretty rough and the temperature was falling every day. January 14, 1943, we arrived at Dutch Harbor, refueled, replenished stores and got underway on the 18th to escort a merchant ship to Constantine Harbor, Amchitka Island. Amchitka was to be our staging point to attack the Japanese who had taken over Kiska, Agattu and Attu Islands.

The Navy Seabees were at work making an air strip to handle attack planes, and Army troops were securing the island and setting up anti-aircraft gun positions. The *Aylwin* was ordered to escort ships carrying troops and material from Adak to Amchitka. We arrived at Constanine Harbor, Amchitka on the 19th of January and after escorting the merchant ship into the harbor, we were assigned a anti-submarine patrol sector outside of the harbor.

Here we were in the middle of winter in the upper latitudes and it was cold. It was just the antithesis of the weather we had become accustomed to experiencing.

Before we left Mare Island we were issued cold weather clothing that included heavy overall type pants, a heavy weather jacket, heavy weather head covering with a face mask and large rubber boots to go over our shoes. We found the most comfortable configuration and warmest for our feet, was to get a size smaller and just wear two pair of socks in the rubber boots.

Shortly after our arrival in the Aleutians, we were ordered to make a trip to Nome, Alaska, about 800 miles north of Dutch Harbor. What a trip this turned out to be. We ran into some storms and the sailing was rough as we battled strong cold winds most of the way up to Nome. When the ship would hit waves it would send showers of spray up all over the front part of the ship and it would freeze on all of the structures.

When we were almost to Dutch Harbor on our return trip, we had a chance to go topside up forward and get a look at our white ghost ship.

It was quite a sight seeing all of the frozen ice covering the whole front of the ship. After refueling, we returned to our patrol station off of Amchitka. This patrol duty turned out to be the most boring experience we encountered during my time aboard the *Aylwin*.

We would just steam along a given track, back and forth, to furnish anti-submarine protection and anti-aircraft fire support. The sun did not rise until mid morning and then it set in mid afternoon.

The only thing that did give us some break in this patrol duty were almost daily air raids by small Japanese float planes which would come over about noontime, and would mess up our noon meal. These planes were small Japanese Zeros that had been fitted with floats and they would carry a 100-pound bomb under each wing. Apparently, they didn't have any bombsights and never did hit anything that I was aware of. We took them under fire with our five-inch guns but we never scored any hits. In talking to the first class firecontrolman, he told us that the optics in the main battery gun director were all frosted up and he couldn't really get a good range on the planes. He had tried everything he could think of and was not able to get rid of the frost. He was afraid to mention it to the gunnery officer for fear of what our new captain would do. So, the Japanese plane would come over, drop his bombs, we would fire away at him and he would fly back to Kiska. We got so used to this that we called him "Washboard Charlie" because of the sound of his engine. Since these daily raids occurred at noontime, our skipper moved the meal times for breakfast and lunch to 10:00 a.m. and 2:00 p.m. respectively.

The captain ordered hot soup and sandwiches be available in the galley 24 hours a day. Some of the men groused about only having two meals a day, but most of us thought it was OK and we didn't suffer any.

Some days, when another ship was on patrol station, we would steam over to Kiska and lob a few five-inch shells at the beach. Again, we had no idea what we were shooting at as the entire island was shrouded in fog, but it made us feel good.

We had no way to get fuel or supplies at Amchitka; every few weeks we would make a trip back to Dutch Harbor or Kodiak Island to refuel. On each of these trips we would also get mail and packages from home. When the fog would clear on one of these trips, the sights were beautiful. The islands in the Aleutian chain were mostly mountains and they were covered with snow and the sky was crystal clear blue. It was so good to see something besides fog.

The Japanese still held the islands of Attu and Agattu. The buildup of an airstrip on Amchitka was part of the plan to retake Kiska, Attu and Agattu. This was to give the U.S. forces close air support.

Through January and February, the *Aylwin* continued to patrol off Constantine Harbor and make trips back to Dutch Harbor to escort cargo ships and to refuel.

On February 18, 1943, we made radar contact with a large group of planes. They turned out to be twelve P-40s that circled over Amchitka.

Soon, we received word that there were two Japanese planes approaching and we went to GQ. The P-40s made quick work in dispatching the two floatplanes.

On March 3, 1943, I was advanced to Radioman Second Class. On March 27, 1943, before the amphibious operations commenced, the *Aylwin* received orders detaching us from the Aleutian operations and directed us to proceed to San Diego.

We proceeded alone arriving at San Diego on April 3, 1943. After entering San Diego harbor, we proceeded to the destroyer base for overhaul and repairs.

The first two days I did not get a chance to go ashore on liberty as factory engineers came aboard to help update the various radars we had installed.

When I did get ashore, it was great to be back in the United States again. San Diego had not changed much since I was here, just before the Pearl Harbor attack, and I spent about two hours just walking some of the downtown streets, taking in the sights.

Later in the week when I was ashore on liberty, I again ran into my good friend Dave Ballard from Topeka, Kansas. We went to a bar and had the following picture taken.

In this photo, starting from the left, Dave is the first, then me, and one of Dave's shipmates from the *Lexington*. Dave was on the *USS Lexington* in the Battle of the Coral Sea and was one of the survivors we picked up when the *Lex* went down. It sure was good to see him again and to get a chance to talk over events of the past year. This was the last time I saw Dave, but I understand that he ended up back east working for RCA as an engineer.

After having repairs at the dockside, the ship moved into dry dock to have the hull scraped and repainted. Even though we had spent most of the time since December 7th underway, there was still a buildup of barnacles and other marine growth below the water line and these resisted the smooth flow of water past the hull when we were underway. This interference of water flow past the hull limited our maximum speed and required more power just to make cruising speed.

After two and a half weeks undergoing repairs and updating equipment, we got underway in company with the *Nassau CVE-16*, an escort aircraft carrier. After completing training exercises, we got underway to join TF 51. The group that we first joined was composed of the battleship *Pennsylvania BB38*, the *Nassau CVE16*, the *Neches AO47*, an oiler and 6 destroyers.

The Task Force that finally rendezvoused on April 16th was composed of three battleships, two troop transports and six destroyers. The Task Force set a north-north-westerly course for the Aleutians.

As we were approaching Amchitka Island one evening, one of the battleships reported radar contact on their fire control radar at a distance of 16,000 yards (eight miles). We checked our air SC-1 search radar and surface search radar, SG, and neither one had any contacts. Checking with our fire control radar, we had a target on that set at 116,000 yards which was a second sweep return signal that appeared on the radar screen as a target at 16,000 yards.

I reported this to the bridge, and suggested that we call the *Pennsylvania* on the TBS ship to ship radio, and tell them that they had a return on the second sweep from Amchitka Island at 116,000 yards. Well, our captain said absolutely not. We were not going to call the task group commander on a battleship and tell him that his ship didn't know how to analyze their radar contacts. The *Pennsylvania* started to fire on their target at 16,000 yards with their main battery guns. We tracked the large projectiles and saw them splash into the ocean at 16,000 yards. By this time all three battleships were firing their main battery guns and it made quite a sight seeing all of those 14 inch projectiles flying through the night sky. After a couple of salvos, we were ordered to proceed at flank speed (maximum) toward their target, and report if we could see anything. When we closed that area, we could still only see splashes of projectiles and reported this to the *Pennsylvania*. The order was then sent for all ships to cease fire. In spite of the fact that the three battleships had been firing on an imaginary target, the task group commander felt that he had not wasted the projectiles as there was no panic, and the entire incident was well carried out. (He was covering his behind.)

Most of April and May 1943 was spent as part of Task Force 51 in the Aleutians, involved in the landing operations centered around Attu Island. The *Aylwin* was involved during most of the operations screening the *Nassau CVE-16*, and serving as plane guard during flight operations. During landing operations on 24-30 May 1943, we provided shore bombardment to cover our troops attacking the Japanese. Some of the time was spent providing submarine patrol off of Attu Island during the landing operations.

The submarine patrols and plane guard during flight operations of the *Nassau* were carried out during most of June 1943. This was very routine duty, and nothing much happened to break up the monotony, other than returning to Adak for fuel and supplies.

The weather was getting much warmer, and we were able to shed the foul weather clothing we wore during the winter months. The food was good, but we missed the get-togethers on the fantail that we had in the South Pacific. I was standing watches in the radio shack and in the radar control room.

The air search and surface search radars were used 24 hours a day, and the surface search (SG) was also used during foggy times for navigation and for station keeping when in company with the carrier.

Since we were not involved in any fighting, the radio circuits were silent most of the time with the exception of the broadcast messages from NPM in Hawaii.

After Attu was retaken, the forces shifted to Kiska Island. In addition to the plane guard detail and anti-submarine patrol, we got a chance to fire our five-inch guns at AA batteries in July 9, 14, 20, and 22. On July 28, we delivered mail and passengers between the *New Mexico, BB40* and the *Mississippi, BB41*. Transferring mail at sea is fairly routine.

We would come up on the stern of one battleship and they would fire a small line over to us, and then we would pull it and a larger line over from the battleship. Attached to this line would be a pulley with a watertight can and a messenger line for pulling the can back and forth. They would put the mail in the can and we would pull it back aboard and remove it from the can. When this was finished, we would untie the main rope and let the battleship take it back aboard with the can and messenger lines.

Transferring personnel between ships at sea is a similar type of operation that utilized a "high line." We would go alongside of the battleship and secure the main line higher up on our ship. Instead of a watertight can, of course, we would use a breeches buoy suspended from a pulley.

The man to be transferred would be secured in the chair and a messenger line would be used to pull the buoy along the main line. During calm seas this procedure was fairly easy, but in rough seas it was touch and go to get the man across without dunking him in the water. On our ship, the main line was passed over a pulley and then down the deck, where about ten or twelve men would hold the line. As the ships would roll apart, these men would run toward the pulley and when the ships came closer they would run back to take up the slack, so that the man in the chair didn't get dunked in the water.

The captain usually had the con during these maneuvers and it was always touch and go keeping our destroyer a constant distance from the larger ship and keeping our speed exactly the same as the larger ship's.

* Photo courtesy of the United States Naval Institute

Transfer Between Ships by Hiline

In all of the months in the Aleutians, we had only one contact on our sonar equipment and, after dropping three 600 pound depth charges, it disappeared. We had almost no radar contacts on Japanese planes, and all of our contacts on the SG surface search radar turned out to be friendly.

On August 31, 1943, we were ordered to escort LST Group 8 with 5 LSTs back to San Francisco. We were all glad to be out of the Aleutians, as the months up there had been really dull and boring. We did get a chance to bombard Kiska Island on several occasions, but most of the months since arriving in January were spent on anti-submarine patrol (ASW) of the various islands under our control, or screening the battleships and cruisers in the area. After all of the action we saw in 1942, the Aleutian campaign was really a drag.

There was one surface action in the Bering Sea in which our destroyers launched a torpedo attack against a Japanese force. However, the *Aylwin* was back at Adak Island getting supplies and fuel when this action took place.

We arrived back at San Francisco on September 11, 1943, and tied up at pier 20S. Since we expected to be in port for about a month, liberty was granted for all hands not having the duty that day. This gave me a chance to get together with my girl Virginia, and it sure was good to see her. We had been exchanging letters for the past five months and we had decided to get married. We had to get permission from the Catholic Church as Virginia was Catholic. Then we had to get blood tests, a license, arrange the ceremony and get the required people to be present. Virginia had no trouble getting her second, as she had her sister Loretta Fischer living with her. I had to go through several fellows before I found a shipmate who wasn't on leave or going on leave.

Finally I got Warren Randall, one of the sonarmen, to stand up as my best man. Everything was finally settled and we were married on September 21, 1943, at St. Brigid's Catholic Church on Van Ness Street in San Francisco.

We were both very happy and in love, and Virginia had made reservations for us at Hobergs Resort, in Lake County, for us to spend our honeymoon. It lasted one week and it sure was great, until we got back to San Francisco. Virginia had to go back to work, and my leave was up. I dropped Virginia off at her apartment and headed back down Market Street to the ship.

I was walking along with my hat sort on the back of my head and my cuffs rolled up on my dress jumper as it was a warm day. About half way down Market, the Shore Patrol pulled up in a Jeep, and I was nailed for not wearing the uniform properly. Of course, the report went back to the ship and I was called up to Captain's Mast.

This is a procedure where the Captain hears what infractions were committed and he assigns punishment. While up in the Aleutians the captain had sworn at me for being too slow in fixing the SG radar. I told him he didn't have to swear at me because I probably came from just as good a family as he did. This really made him hopping mad, and he was just waiting for me to step out of line once, so he could get back at me. This was his chance, and he made the most of it, restricting me to the ship for a week. At the same Captain's Mast was one of the seaman who the police had brought back to the ship for fighting in the street with a woman. The captain let him off with just a warning. So goes Navy justice.

On October 11, 1943, Commandeer R.O. Strange relieved Commander Malpass as Commanding Officer of the *Aylwin*.

This tour in the Aleutians proved to be much more interesting than our previous tours, as we did get chances to bombard Kiska more often, and to support the amphibious landings on Attu Island. When our troops made landings at Attu and Agattu, they found no Japanese troops left, but there was ground fighting on Kiska.

As I said before, we were in Adak when the battle took place in the Bering Sea. We all wished we could have been there to take part, but after exchanging several salvos, the Japanese retired and were not sighted again in the area, so we didn't miss out on much. None of our ships were damaged and neither were any of the Japanese vessels.

10

The Gilbert Islands

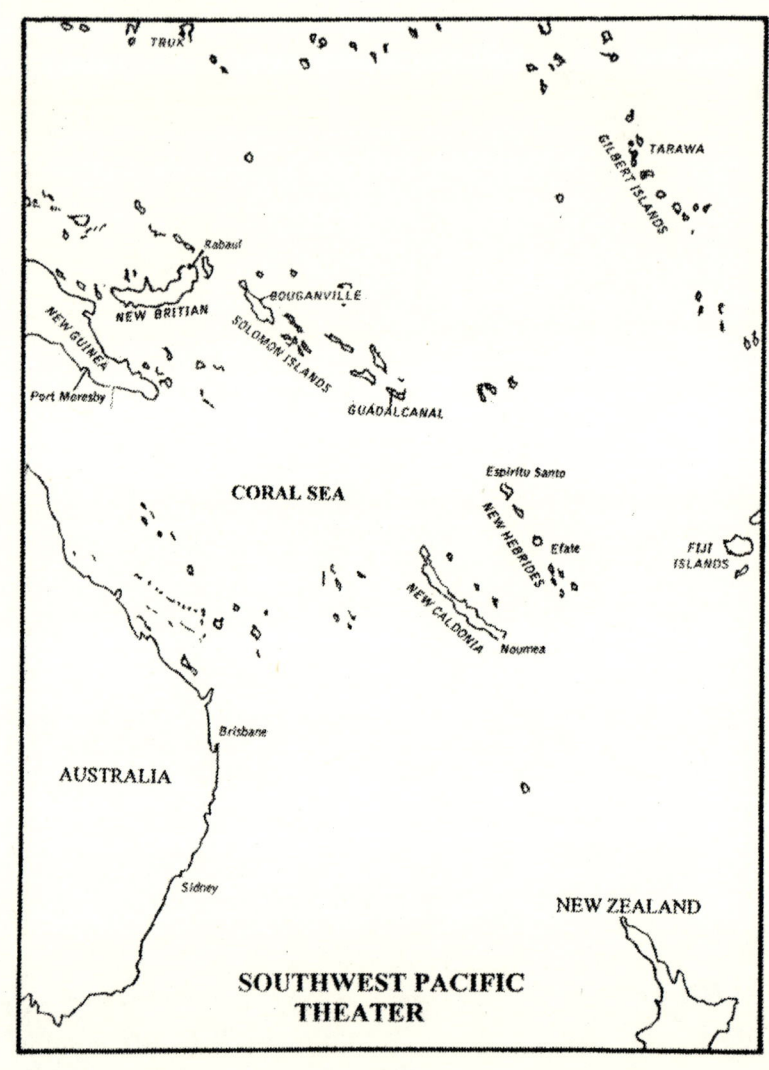

Tarawa Atoll is one of the Gilbert Islands, and is shown in the upper right corner of this map.

Things were looking up for a us on the *Aylwin*, as our tour of duty in the Aleutians was behind us. We had a new skipper who appeared to be a real good officer. We had returned to San Francisco on September 11th, 1943 and tied up to pier #54 and then to pier #20.

From there, we went into the Navy Yard at Mare Island for repairs. When we were ready to leave the Navy Yard, there was a civilian engineer on board making adjustments to our fire control radar. The captain sent down word that the engineer had better leave the ship, as we would not be making any stops in the Bay area, and we would be heading out to sea. The engineer said that he would catch the pilot boat as the pilot left our ship. He didn't know that we were leaving with other destroyers, and only the lead ship had a pilot on board. When we passed under the Golden Gate Bridge he went to the bridge to find out when the pilot would be leaving, and found that he couldn't get off. Since he was an engineer, the *Aylwin* put him up in one of the officer's rooms and he stayed with us until we arrived in Espiritu Santo. I saw him after we arrived as he was leaving the ship. He said that when we arrived, all of his bags and tools were there with a letter from his boss saying, "Congratulations, you are now our representative in the South West Pacific."

The *Aylwin* departed California on October 19, 1943, and headed southwest, in company with her sister ships, the *Farragut DD348* and the *Monaghan DD354*. On the 20th, we joined three carriers, the *Sangamon CVE26*, the *Chenango CVE28* and the *Suwannee CVE27*. Just before we departed, I was informed that the Navy had established a new rate of Radio Technician, and I was advanced from 2nd Class Radioman to 1st Class Radio Technician.

On our trip south, we exercised antiaircraft fire at sleeves towed by planes from the carriers, and the carriers carried out daily aircraft exercises with one of the destroyers acting as plane guard. On two of the days, we rescued crewmembers from two TBF bombers that crashed in the water, and transferred them back to the carriers when we refueled at sea from the carriers.

The weather was getting much warmer, and it was really good topside. We were getting into the area where the sunrises and sunsets were so beautiful, and we got a chance to see them each day, because we were still going to battle stations (GQ) an hour before sunrise, and again at sunset.

After the evening meal, we again were able to go back on the fantail to enjoy the music at least until sunset when the GQ alarm would sound. Even though we had good surface search radar that could pick up submarine periscopes, we were still most vulnerable at these times to submarine attacks. The periscope did not make a very good target, just sticking up a couple of feet above the surface of the water, and if the surface of the water was rough, that made it very difficult to detect a thin periscope. I was standing watches on the SG surface search radar while training new operators. The SG console was located in what used to be the Captain's sea cabin, just behind the pilot house on the bridge deck. When not watching the scopes on the SG, I would go into the pilot house and talk to the first class signalman who would be standing watch on the bridge deck. When we got to talking about families, he told me that he was married to a retired call girl from Honolulu. This really took me back a bit, because I couldn't imagine being married to a call girl. But, he claimed that they were very happy, and he didn't have to worry about her stepping out on him, now that she was retired from that activity.

We were again in the area where the Pacific was a beautiful blue color, and watching it as we sailed by had a calming and soothing effect on us. Even though it was the same water we had seen in the Aleutians, up there it seemed cold and foreboding and we just didn't feel like spending any time looking at it.

We headed south-west for Espiritu Santo Island to pick up cruisers and troop transports for Operation Galvanic, the invasion in the Gilbert Islands. Espiritu Santo is the largest island in the New Hebrides Islands, about 500 miles west of Fiji and 1,100 miles east of Australia. The location of Espiritu Santo can be seen on the map of the Southwest Pacific at the beginning of this chapter. It is located just to the right, and just above, the center of the map. The Gilbert Islands are located at the top right area of the map.

We used Espiritu Santo as the jumping off point for attacking the Solomon Island chain and other Japanese occupied islands in that area. On November 5th, we arrived at Espiritu Santo and, after refueling from a tanker, we anchored in Turtle Bay. While at anchor a boat delivered a newspaper correspondent who would be sailing with us for the next operation. Those of us in the radio shack got to know him quite well, as he used us to transmit his stories back to land. This was an eye-opening experience for me, because what he would describe in his reports sounded like fiction to those of us who had seen everything he was reporting.

Guadalcanal was now secure and the U.S. Navy needed to start offensive operations to attack the Japanese in the Central Pacific. It was decided to strike the Gilbert Islands with attacks by the U.S. Marines on Tarawa and U.S. Army troops on Makin Atoll. These attacks were scheduled to start on November 20, 1943.

In overall command of the amphibious operations was Admiral Richmond Turner, and his deputy, Admiral Harry Hill, was in charge of Task Force 53, which was to make landings on Tarawa Atoll.

In addition to the troop ships, TF 53 also had a bombardment group to support the landings. It was composed of five escort carriers for air support, three battleships, five cruisers and twenty-one destroyers, of which the *Aylwin* was one.

In charge of the Marines was General Holland M. (Howling Mad) Smith. He had claimed that he could out shout any Navy admiral. On D-Day minus 1, the battleships and cruisers started bombardment of Betio Island on Tarawa Atoll, with carrier planes from our task group also attacking Japanese gun emplacements and pillboxes. The devastation that we could see from our position about ten miles from the atoll was complete, as far as we could tell. It didn't seem possible that anything could be alive on Betio after that furious assault. It had lasted all day long. On the morning of D-Day, November 20,1943, the bombardment continued until the troops started their approach to the island.

Betio Island was typical of many of the Central Pacific atoll islands, in that it was surrounded by coral reefs that extended some distance from the beaches on the island. These reefs had to be penetrated in order to make it to the beach and onto the land.

The amphibious landings in the Solomon Islands did not have these reefs to contend with, and the Navy had been using LCVP (landing craft vehicle personnel), known as *Higgins Boats*, to carry the troops from the troop transports to the beaches.

Knowing that they needed to be able to penetrate the coral reefs, a small group of Marine and Navy officers designed a boat that had tracks and a propeller. This boat, the LVT-1 (landing vehicle tracked), was known as the *Alligator*, and it was to get its first trial in combat at Betio.

Unfortunately, the tides at Betio were at low ebb when the landing vehicles arrived and some of the reefs were exposed above the water line making penetration or passage over them difficult, if not impossible, at some of the planned landing sites.

These reefs extended quite some distance from the island and out to about a half a mile at points. As the *Higgins boats* and *Alligators* arrived with their Marines, they had to unload their troops on the reefs where they were exposed to murderous machine gun and mortar fire from pillboxes on the island.

The LVT-1s suffered from not giving much protection to the embarked troops. Out of 125 that were used during the assault, only 35 survived, and many of them were badly damaged. From lessons learned at Betio, new LVT-2s were employed in future amphibious operations, which provided much better protection for embarked troops. The carnage at Tarawa Atoll cost the Americans 1,009 dead and 2,101 wounded, a casualty rate of more than 17% of the 18,000 Marines who assaulted Betio Island.

The Japanese troops had gone underground in caves during the bombardments, so many survived the fight on D-Day.

One item of interest in the landing operations at Betio Island, that has not had much publicity, is worth mentioning here. Eddie Albert, the TV and movie actor, was attached to one of the troop transports as a LT, USNR during this operation. He led some of the *Higgins boats* on the initial assault, and when he found an opening in the reef, he stationed himself at that point and guided other boats past the reef and into the beach.

During the afternoon, we approached the island and gave fire support to the Marines who were storming the beaches. I could see what a hard time they were having, because the island looked almost bare with no objects for our guys to take shelter behind.

To provide air cover and other needed support, Task Force 50, under Admiral Spruance, of Midway fame, was operating in the area to ward off any attack by the Japanese Imperial Fleet. That task force was composed of six new large carriers, five light carriers, six battle ships, eight cruisers and twenty-one destroyers. These ships were divided up into four task groups. The U.S. Navy now had more carriers and other large combat ships than the Japanese Imperial Navy had at its disposal.

After finishing our fire support to the Marines, we again functioned as a screen for the carriers as the mop-up operations were carried on in the Gilberts. December 8, 1943, we received orders to escort the *USS Maryland, BB46* back to Pearl Harbor, arriving there on December 14,1943.

In company with the carriers and the *Maryland*, the *Aylwin* proceeded to a Radar Picket Station about 10 miles ahead of the formation. This was a new concept for early warning of approaching aircraft in that it extended the radar coverage by an additional 10 miles from the formation.

We only stayed in Pearl Harbor overnight and got underway on December 15th for San Francisco, escorting three battleships to San Francisco. We arrived in San Francisco Bay on December 21st, and proceeded to Alameda for repairs and liberty. It sure was great to be home again with Virginia for Christmas.

It was not as good for one of the other sailors. As soon as he got ashore, he went to a bus stop and while waiting for a bus, another man asked him, "Haven't I seen you before?" Well, he had seen him alright, and the last time he had seen him, they got into a fight. So it started all over again, and our sailor ended up in jail and was restricted to the ship for the rest of our stay in Alameda.

December 29th, we were underway again for San Diego, escorting the same three battleships we were in company with from Pearl Harbor to San Francisco. We arrived in San Diego on December 30th, and ended the year 1943 tied up in San Diego Harbor alongside the *Farragut*, *Monaghan*, and the *Dale*, all destroyers of Destroyer Squadron 1 (DESRON1).

11

The Marshall Islands

While tied up in San Diego, we knew something big was in the planning stages. On January 1, 1944, the other destroyers in our squadron got underway in the morning and stood out to sea. Then in the afternoon, we got underway and joined up with five LSTs (Landing Ship Tank) and a new command ship.

* Photo courtesy of U.S. Navy Department -Naval Historical Center

LST

We proceeded to San Clemente Island to conduct training exercises. These exercises continued for four days in conjunction with some LCIs (Landing Craft Infantry), where the procedures for conducting landings were rehearsed on San Clemente Island. Upon completion we returned to San Diego Harbor and anchored for the night.

January 6, 1944 the *Aylwin* was ordered to get underway and escort five LSTs and two YMS (Motor Mine Sweeps) to Kauai.

The YMS were only about 100 feet long and during the crossing we ran into some rather rough water. The small YMS kept disappearing from our SG radar screen and from visual sighting. They would go out of sight as they went into a trough of a wave, and then reappear as they rode the crest of the next wave. It was a little rough riding on our destroyer but those poor guys on those little YMSs were sure having a real struggle just trying to stay alive. With these landing ships and YMSs, our speed varied from 6 to 9 knots for this trip. Our usual cruising speed is 15 -18 knots, so this trip took over twice as long as the usual crossing to the islands. We finally arrived at Nawiliwili Harbor, Kauai, TH and the LSTs anchored. The *Aylwin* got underway and proceeded to Pearl Harbor where we tied up at the fuel dock and awaited further orders.

We returned to Kauai and patrolled offshore until about noon of January 20, 1944, at which time we were joined by five LSTs and two SCs (Sub Chasers) and we proceeded southwest toward the Marshall Islands. The LSTs had to fuel the SCs and we had to furnish them with fresh water during the trip west.

* Photo courtesy of U.S. Navy Department -Naval Historical Center

Sub Chaser

These sub-chasers were even smaller than the YMS that we escorted to Kauai. When the sea got rough, the poor little guys would disappear from site as they went into the valley between waves, and then reappear as they rode the crest of the next wave. The ride on a destroyer can get pretty rough at times but nothing like these little boats.

Our executive officer had let those of us in the radio shack see the operation plan for the coming actions, since we needed to know the communication setup.

This plan was titled Operation Flintlock. It covered the attacks we were going to conduct against the Japanese forces in the Marshall Islands. Our task group was to be part of the assault on Kwajalein Atoll in the Marshall Island group.

Kwajalein Atoll is a coral formation in the western chain of the Marshall Islands. It is a string of 90 islets, and has a total area of six square miles that surround the world's largest lagoon at 655 square miles.

We arrived at Kwajalein on January 30th, in time to see some of the battle ships and cruisers bombarding the island. The island was also under heavy bombardment from carrier planes that seemed to constantly come in to drop their bombs. They pounded the island until it seemed that nothing could still be alive.

This was much heavier bombardment than was carried out at Tarawa Atoll. Since the casualty toll was so high at Tarawa, Admiral Kelly Turner insisted on a much heavier bombardment at Kwajalein.

The troop transports had anchored in the lagoon where they discharged their troops on to LVCP (Higgins boats) and LVTs (amtracks) for the trip to the beach.

These boats would form circles and as soon as the bombardments were finished they would break up the circles, and proceed to the beach.

That afternoon, we entered the lagoon and covered the LSTs that were anchored there waiting to move onto the beach from the lagoon side and unload their tanks and trucks. While waiting, we received a message from the LST 119 that their radar was out and could the

Aylwin send over a technician to help them. Of course our skipper said yes, and I was told to get my equipment and tools together and stand by. The deck crew lowered our motor whaleboat and I had to go down a chain ladder to board the boat that then took me over to the LST.

When I first got aboard I found a radar system that I had never seen, so it took longer than we expected to find the problem and get it running again. While we were working, the LST made its landing on the beach to discharge its cargo. So, I made a landing on Kwajalein during the D-Day operations. After seeing the LST make its landing, the *Aylwin* sent their motor whaleboat over to get me back, so my part of the landing party was over. I was actually in no danger as there were no Japanese on the beach area where we landed. However, it was an experience that most destroyer sailors never get a chance to enjoy.

From February 2nd through the 6th, we patrolled offshore to guard against submarines. We then went to Majuro Atoll, Marshall Islands, where we refueled and took on provisions during the 8th and 9th of February. While we were anchored in the lagoon we were tied up next to another destroyer.

In the evening, when it was time to show a movie, we had only one projector and if we were anchored alone, the operator would have to stop at the end of each reel and rewind. When we tied up alongside another destroyer, we would share the screen and then each ship would furnish a projector so we could see the whole show without a wait between reels.

Taking on provisions and ammunition on a destroyer is an all-hands job. Everyone from all divisions of the ship turns to and gives a hand loading cargo. I got a real charge seeing the sailors from the engineering department carrying boxes of canned foods. When they would get a box of canned fruit, or something else that was good, they would drop one box down the engine room hatch for their own private stock. Replenishing food stores and ammunition was long and backbreaking work and it would usually take a full day, so all of us would really get tired from working in the hot sun.

During one of our stays in Majuro lagoon we entered a floating dry-dock to scrape the hull below the water line. This was a dirty and lengthy job and all hands "turned to" in helping get all of the barnacles and other growth removed from the hull. The barnacles and other marine growth increased the friction with the sea and slowed us down, so periodically we would have to get it removed and have the hull repainted

On February 15th, we joined several other destroyers in a screen for three battleships enroute to Eniwetok Atoll, in the western Marshall Islands. After the task group had assumed its course we were ordered to proceed ahead and assume the radar picket station. This station was 10 to 12 miles ahead of the formation in the direction the task group was traveling.

Of course life aboard our ship goes on, following the same daily routine of standing watches, going to battle stations twice a day, sleeping (when we can), working, doing our laundry, taking showers and eating. We usually would get a shower every day. We always had clean clothes and we got three square meals a day. The Marines on the other hand had to fight their way ashore, dig trenches for protection, wear the same clothes for days and even weeks and only get a square meal occasionally. You can now see why I joined the Navy.

We sighted Eniwetok Atoll, on the morning of February 17, 1944 and the *Aylwin* proceeded to a patrol area while the battleships and cruisers entered the lagoon to take up shore bombardment positions. Later in the day we entered the lagoon and anchored for the night. The next morning we were assigned to patrol the ocean side of the entrance to the lagoon. As we were leaving the entrance channel between two islands, one of the battleships had the island on our starboard side under bombardment with their sixteen inch guns.

This put us on a course that was parallel with the sixteen inch projectiles. As we approached the island on our starboard side we could look out the port hole and see these projectiles tearing up all of the palm trees and installations and landing out in the ocean beyond the island. They sounded like a high speed train roaring by and it made quite a deafening noise as they sailed by. When we cleared the channel, we had to call the battleship and request that they cease firing as their projectiles were landing in our assigned patrol area.

Later in the afternoon, we were assigned to a picket station 25 to 30 miles south of the atoll. On February 21st, we bombarded Parry Island in the Eniwetok Atoll to destroy Japanese positions on Parry.

A day later, we left Eniwetok to escort LSTs back to Kwajalein Atoll arriving there on February 26th, and then returning to Eniwetok in company with two cruisers.

On March 7^{th,} the *Aylwin* and other destroyers of Squadron One were detached and ordered to proceed to Majuro Atoll arriving there on March 13th, where we all went alongside the destroyer tender *Prairie* for repairs and upkeep. While there, we converted the Chart Room, that was one deck below the bridge, into a Combat Information Center (CIC).

In the early stages of the war at sea, the captain of a ship would decide what his next course of action would be based on his own assessment of all of the data available. His judgement was based on what he could see through his own eyes and reports from others, such as lookouts, other officers on the bridge and reports from the radio room.

However, as technology continued to produce new equipment to detect more data on the enemy, a captain had to rely on many sources of information to find out what was going on.

With the development of air search radar, surface search radar, fire control radar, sonar and very high frequency (VHF) radio equipment for communicating with other ships and aircraft, a captain could not be expected to be able to analyze all of this information by himself. The need to provide a captain with quick analysis of all of the information led to the development of a Combat Information Center (CIC) on each ship.

The *Aylwin* already had the above radar and sonar equipment, and the tender installed VHF radio equipment that would give us the capability of contacting the carrier aircraft. We would also have a Fighter Director Officer (FDO) who would be capable of controlling aircraft while we were on radar picket station.

A Radar Picket Station of a fast carrier task force when getting ready to attack would be located about fifty miles from the task force in the direction of the expected attack or target.

When the carrier planes would be launched for an attack, they would be vectored over the picket station where we would then give them a vector to the target. After the attack, the planes would check in overhead of the picket station.

Our FDO would be stationed on the deck above the bridge deck with a VFH radio outlet, to give our returning planes a vector back to the carriers. The FDO would also make a visual check to make sure that there were no Japanese planes shadowing our returning planes.

When we left Majuro Atoll on March 22, 1944, we joined Task Force 52, composed of four task groups. Each task group had two new *Essex* carriers, new light carriers built from cruiser hulls, new battleships, five to six cruisers and a screen of destroyers. When this entire task force was finally assembled, I went up to the director deck above the bridge deck to take a look. As far as I could see were all of the combat ships of the task force with a total of eight new large carriers.

Having been through the Battle of the Coral Sea where we only had two large carriers, and the Battle of Midway where we only had three carriers to the Japanese's six, this was a sight to behold. It took my breath away to see so much power all in one task force. I was now confident that we would surely win the Pacific War against Japan with so much power at hand. My confidence level and my feelings of security were now at an all-time high.

We still had many more Japanese bases on other islands to attack and take over, but I knew that we would surely win in the end with all of these new carriers, battleships, cruisers, destroyers and support ships. It was exhilarating and sure made us proud to be a part of such great task force.

12

The Caroline Islands

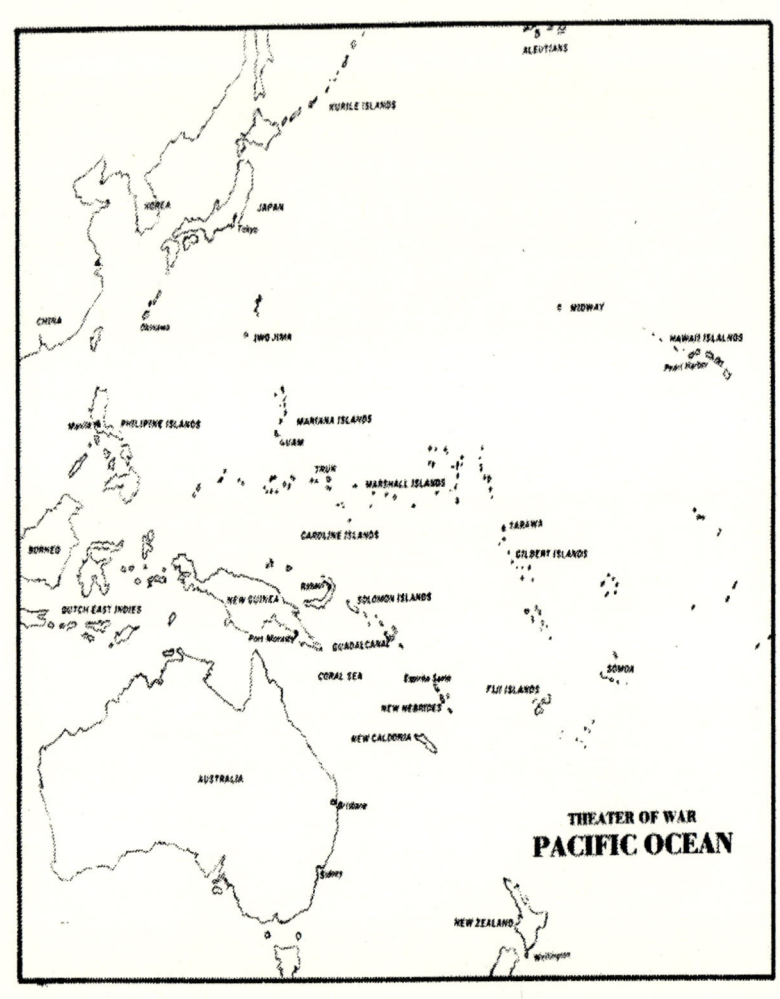

Caroline Islands

The Fifth Fleet was under the command of Admiral Raymond Spruance of Midway fame and he had at his disposal some 375 ships, 700 carrier aircraft and 475 land-based aircraft. His mission was to land 53,000 assault troops in the Caroline Islands.

The Caroline Islands are an archipelago in the western Pacific Ocean and were occupied and fortified by the Japanese. They included Ponape, Truk, Yap and Palau, with Truk having Japan's largest and strongest installations, including a fairly large airstrip and a large lagoon for fleet anchorage. It was called "The Gibraltar of the Pacific."

Admiral Nimitz had decided to bypass Truk and concentrate on taking Palau and Yap. Since the fortifications on Truk were so extensive and well-garrisoned, our losses would have been unacceptable. Our plans were to neutralize the Japanese Naval Air Force on Truk with carrier strikes from Task Group 58.2 and then to proceed to take Palau and Yap.

Enroute from Majuro to the Caroline Islands we held sunrise and sunset General Quarters (GQ) each day. On March 26, 1944, Task Group 58.2 was joined by tankers for refueling all of the ships in the force.

As we neared Truk on March 29th, we made radar contact on an air raid closing, and all ships went to general quarters. The carriers launched their fighters to form a Combat Air Patrol (CAP), which intercepted the raid, shooting down a number and chasing off the rest. On the *Aylwin*, we never did see any of the Japanese planes and we secured from GQ about an hour later.

On March 30th, we were about 75 miles from Palau and the Task Group launched planes for bombing and strafing attacks on Palau.

After sunrise GQ, we remained at battle stations for the morning.

In the early afternoon we recovered the crew of an SBC2C dive-bomber which we had to ditch in the water due to damage. The plane stayed afloat for a minute or so and the crew had a chance to inflate their rubber raft and get into it before the plane sank. When we came alongside to recover the crew, they hadn't even gotten wet. Shortly after that, Japanese planes were sighted coming in just over the water, thereby avoiding radar detection until they were in visual range from the screening destroyers.

A Zero fighter, which was flying at about 10 to 15 feet above the water, was coming between the *Aylwin* and a cruiser which was on our port beam and we both had it under fire with 20mm and 40mm antiaircraft guns.

As I looked out, it seemed to me that when the plane came directly between our two ships we would be firing directly at each other. Just before the plane reached that point, both ships connected and the plane blew up. Another close action and we had not taken a hit of any kind yet.

No ships in Task Group 58.2 were hit during the attack which was driven off by antiaircraft gunfire. A number of the attacking planes were destroyed by the AA fire and those that escaped were shot down by our CAP.

After the raid on Truk Island, and the carrier attacks on Yap and Palau, the *Aylwin* was ordered to come alongside the *New Jersey* and receive a message to be transmitted back to Pearl Harbor.

We were then ordered to proceed independently to Manus Island that is located in the Admiralty Islands, and transmit the message from that location. We proceeded at full speed and arrived about 1:00 a.m. in the morning and transmitted the message to Pearl Harbor.

While returning from Manus we ran into a typhoon with winds up to 100 mph and waves as high as 30 to 50 feet. This was quite a roller coaster ride as we would just get to the top of one wave and then we would come crashing down into the next trough.

As we would crest over the top of a wave, the screws would come out of the water and the whole aft end of the ship would vibrate until the screws would go into the water again. While this was going on, the ship would bend in the mid section and I wondered how long it could hold together. Of course, we were also rolling from side to side about 45 to 50 degrees. It was quite a ride and I'll never forget it and I certainly would not want another ride like it.

After that we returned to Task Group 58.2 as previously directed. TG 58.2 then returned to Majuro Atoll where we anchored in the lagoon for about a week. While anchored, we did repair work to the radar, sonar and radio equipment. The lagoon was not very deep and we could look down and see all kinds of fish and other marine life. After our work was done, we finally got permission to go swimming over the side. The water was nice and warm and so clear, that it was amazing how much we could see underwater.

We tried diving into the lagoon from the bridge deck, about 25 feet above the water. After that we would see who could swim under the ship and come up on the other side the fastest. We had a great time swimming all afternoon.

I had mentioned earlier that the ship had changed my rate from Radioman to Radio Technician First Class. They had done that because I was doing maintenance and trouble shooting on all of the radio, radar and sonar equipment on board.

When it was time for my advancement to chief, we found out that I could not make Chief Radio Technician, since I did not have the nine months Radio Material School at the Naval Research Laboratory. Our Executive Officer, LT B. H. Britten, talked to the chiefs and requested that I be moved to the chief's quarters so that the bridge could call me by phone. Then, the bridge would not have to send the boatswains mate of the watch back to the petty officers' compartment in the aft part of the ship to get me.

The chiefs all agreed, and I was glad to make the move, as the bunks in these quarters were really good and the chow was much better. The chiefs had their own refrigerator and they kept it stocked with all kinds of food.

The exec told the Chief Fire Controlman, Worrell, and me that since we could not be advanced any further in the enlisted ranks, he and the captain had decided to recommend us for warrant officers. That night, Worrell and I were talking at the table in the chief's quarters during the mid watch (midnight - 4 a.m.), and he asked me if I wanted a drink. He went to the refrigerator, got out a can of orange juice and poured each of us a glass. He then went to his locker and came out with a can of alcohol that he added to the orange juice. It was a great drink for a couple of sailors who had been away from any bar for such a long time. He then told me that the Chief Torpedoman had taken some of the torpedo juice and distilled it and given him a little. Another night, a young chief in the chief's quarters told me that he had gotten his girlfriend in Boston pregnant. When he said that they should get married, she told him she wouldn't marry him if he was the last man on earth. This surprised me, because I had never run into a person who had this experience before.

The next day we went into a floating dry dock. They pumped the water out and raised the whole dock up to the water line which left us high and dry.

We all had to pitch in and scrape the barnacles off of the bottom and clean the sonar dome and the fathom-meter cover.

Then the whole bottom was sand blasted and repainted with anti-fouling pain. By evening we were all bushed and ready for a shower, dinner and bed.

After we got out of dry dock, we got a chance to see some more movies, and most important we got mail from home delivered. It sure was great to hear from somebody other than the boatswain mate passing the word.

It was not all work during this time in the lagoon. We were granted liberty to one of the small islands that form the outer rim of the lagoon. It didn't look too inviting but I decided to give it a try, just to see what it was like on one of these islands.

We loaded aboard our whale boat for the trip ashore and when we arrived the coxswain told us he would be back in four hours to pick us up again. This island was only about twenty yards wide and maybe a hundred yards long. There was nothing there but sand and some palm trees.

Someone higher up in the taskforce had arranged this liberty and had provided many cans of beer. I sampled one and it was warm and tasted awful so that was the end of any drinking. We did go for a short swim but we hadn't brought any swimsuits and it just didn't feel right skinny dipping. So, we just tried to find some shade under the palm trees to stay out of the sun while we told sea stories. We got sunburned so it wasn't one of my better liberties during WWII. It felt good to get back to the ship, take a cool shower and get some clean clothes.

At the end of our week at anchor, the Task Force received orders to get underway and proceed to New Guinea to support the landings at Hollandia and Humboldt Bay by the South Pacific amphibious forces. (Since the orders for this operation were for just a short time, the New Guinea action will be covered here rather than making a separate chapter for it.)

While enroute south, the electronic coding machine (ECM) broke down and the only personnel authorized to look at it or use it were the commissioned officers. None of them had any technical training or experience, so the captain asked Worrell and me to take a look at it and see if we could fix the problem. We took the ECM from the coding room to the ship's office where they had three desks in a line. This would give us a long work space.

We started taking the machine apart, laying the parts in a line as we disconnected them so we would know what order to reconnect everything. We finally came to a camshaft that looked like it was worn too far. We drew up a sketch of what it should look like and took it to the machinist mate to have a replacement made.

When the new part arrived, we put the machine back together, tested it out, and it worked just fine. The Exec put me on the coding board, and since I knew the Morse code, I was given the job of trying to find out what was wrong with garbled messages.

I would try to figure out which letters in the key code group the radioman had made a mistake copying. It was fun and the captain was pleased that we were getting more messages that were readable.

During the trip south, destroyers took turns serving as radar picket

151

ships. We took our turn several times and it was good duty as we didn't have to keep station as closely as we did on the antisubmarine screen. The radar pickets were now just ten miles ahead of the task force. Since the *Aylwin* burned less fuel than some of the newer destroyers, we were called upon to serve in a number of different assignments in the task force.

We were usually designated as the plane guard for one of the carriers as flight operations were carried on a very high speed and destroyers would burn a lot of fuel leaving a screening station and going to plane guard duty astern of the carrier. We were also picked to transfer personnel or messages between the larger ships.

One evening as the task force was changing course, our captain was on the bridge and he took over the con. He ordered the helmsman to apply right standard rudder, and then he and the officer of the deck started to argue about which course to take to get to our new position. This discussion went on for quite a while as the ship continued to turn in a circle and the captain didn't remember his order to the helmsman. (This is almost the same thing that happened to Captain Queeg in the *Cain Mutiny*.) Shortly, the TBS radio came on and the screen commander wanted to know what we were doing. When the captain found out what was happening, he ordered the helmsman off of the bridge and he was never to return to the bridge. This man was our first class quartermaster, and he was our best helmsman on board. Later, the exec talked to the captain, and he admitted that it was his mistake and soon our good helmsman was back on the job.

As we approached Hollandia, we picked up incoming aircraft on the radar while on picket station. The attacking Japanese planes flew right over us and did not even give us a look. Of course, they were only interested in the carriers and couldn't be bothered with a little destroyer. We did not fire any of our guns as the only attack by the Japanese on TF 58 were by aircraft and our CAP took care of them. Again we had to refuel from time to time and it was like getting a drink when we were thirsty.

As I said before, my battle station since joining TF 58 was

operating the fire control radar. This radar was located up in the main battery director on the deck above the bridge deck. This was actually the highest point on the ship manned by anyone during GQ.

The convertible top was never up while we were at battle stations. This position gave us a great view of everything going on in the task force — it was just like having a deluxe box seat at a 49ers game.

To maintain radio silence, messages and orders to the ships in the task force were sent by flashing light. They used the same Morse code used in radio communication. Our gunnery officer knew the code and he and I would have a contest to see which one would be the first to read the signals. In addition to seeing everything, we also could get inside information by reading the signals. It was great fun and it sure broke up just sitting and waiting for something to happen and not knowing what was going on.

The *Aylwin* received orders one afternoon to enter Hollandia Bay at nighttime and take Japanese positions under fire. After nightfall we entered the harbor and started bombarding Japanese positions.

We navigated using the SG radar and used the FD fire control radar for ranging. We finally got return fire and carefully plotted all of their gun positions from the flashes. This information was passed on to the Marines so that they would know where the Japanese guns were.

They did not score any hits on us that night and, when we were finished plotting all of their gun positions, we made our way out of the harbor at flank speed.

After completing the support of landings in New Guinea, the task force headed back to the Caroline Islands for another raid on Truk Island.

When we arrived in the area where TG 58.2 was to launch attacks, we met tankers and refueling operations were started. While the refueling was going on 15 zero fighters attacked TG58.2. Some of the zeros were shot down by antiaircraft fire and those that got away were dispatched by our F6F fighters. Again, the poor sailors on the tankers looked really scared during the attack, probably due to this being their first experience in a shooting action. Maybe we were getting too cocky and over-confident, but after our experiences in 1942 and '43, we didn't feel we had much to worry about in a small air attack.

Before this air attack, we had been sitting up on the fo'c'sle deck. We had been sitting there reading and suddenly flying fish started landing on the deck next to us. I had no idea that they could jump that high, but there they were. They would lay on the deck and flip around trying to get back to the water. As fast as I could, I would scoop them up and throw them back in the water. They just kept jumping up on the deck, so I had to give up reading for awhile.

This completed operations in the Caroline Islands and we headed back to Majuro.

13

The Mariana Islands

The Mariana Islands

After the last raid on Truk Island and the successful taking of Yap and Palau Islands, Task Force 58 returned to Majuro Atoll to anchor in the lagoon and conduct ship repairs, replenishment of stores and training exercises.

The *Aylwin* went alongside the *Prairie*, a destroyer tender to get needed repairs. After receiving some of the needed work, the ship entered a floating dry dock to get repairs to the underwater hull. This was another all-hands effort in that we all had to help scrape the underwater hull. It sure was a dirty job. After a few days in the dry dock, we returned to alongside the *Prairie* and other destroyers to carry on ships force repair and maintenance of equipment. This time in the lagoon at Majuro was also utilized for underway training, both in navigation and antiaircraft firing. We would get underway and conduct exercises in the ocean near Majuro with a few other ships. Antiaircraft firings were conducted on towed sleeves while underway at sea. This period at Majuro lasted for the month of May 1944. It was an enjoyable period as we did not have General Quarters every morning and evening at sunrise and sunset. In the radio shack we still needed to copy the broadcast transmissions from Pearl Harbor, but we took turns with the other ships in the nest of destroyers so that we could completely shut down the radio shack on the days we didn't have the watch. We got a chance to catch up on sleep, get some letters written and get in some time swimming. The weather was nice and warm but not too hot and it was ideal sleeping up on deck at night after the movies. After a couple of weeks we had seen all of the movies in the area, but we still enjoyed seeing them again.

We finally got underway from Majuro on June 6th with other ships of Task Force 58 for attacks on the Mariana Islands. The Mariana Islands are a group of volcanic craters in the western Pacific about 1,500 miles east of the Philippines composed of Saipan, Tinian Rota and Guam. Guam was a territory of the United States, whereas the northern islands in the chain have been occupied by Japan since 1914. The U.S. forces needed the northern islands for airfields to conduct B-29 bomber strikes against Japanese home islands.

Flight operations were conducted enroute and, of course, we were back on regular watches and other underway routines.

Seven days later, we arrived just off of Saipan Island and the *Aylwin* was assigned to the northern bombardment group with the battle ship *South Dakota*. The *South Dakota* was assigned targets inland, while we had to close the beach and support the marines with close in targets. It was a busy time as we started receiving return fire from the Japanese shore batteries. Again, we were leading charmed lives as we received no hits. The following day, the task group refueled and took up position screening the transports that were anchored just off shore of Saipan.

While patrolling we were attacked by high altitude bombers and low flying torpedo planes. All ships opened up and after shooting down several planes the Japanese planes retired. None of our ships were hit and again we felt pretty lucky. I should mention again that destroyers are so narrow that they do not make much of a target for attack from aircraft and we do not represent as major a threat as the carriers do. Knowing this, we really didn't have much fear during air attacks at this stage of the war. It was still an exciting time when air raids occurred and it gave us a chance to see the Japanese air forces being cut down in size.

During this period around Saipan Island, while the landing operations were being conducted, we were under air attacks almost daily, however none of the ships in Task Force were hit. We were on picket patrol almost every other day and about every third day we would refuel from tankers or one of the large ships in the Task Force. After the island of Saipan was secured our task group shifted its target to Guam.

The *Aylwin* was part of the shore bombardment group assigned the task of softening up the beaches in Guam.

* Photo courtesy of the United States Naval Institute

Aylwin Firing on Guam

After a couple of days, the transports moved in and the marines started landing operations. We could look over and see the amtracks and Higgins boats landing on the beaches. After a short while, the whole area of the beaches was covered by a cloud of dust. Our carrier planes were making bombing attacks and there was gunfire support from our task group. It was hot and dirty ashore and our guys were under intense fire. We sure felt sorry for our marines having to exist under those conditions. We were busy furnishing 5-inch fire support, but when we got a break, we could get a nice meal and a shower.

At night the marines needed star shell illumination, so we would approach the beach as closely as we could and steam parallel to the beach with just enough headway to maintain course and fire a star shell about every two or three minutes. At the end of a run of about

2,000 yards we would cease firing, reverse course, and then start firing again. This reversing of course would take about five to ten minutes and things would be silent.

Those of us off watch would be sleeping below decks. We got used to the gun going off every couple of minutes and we seemed to sleep right through it. However, when the ship reached the end of the 2,000 yard track and ceased firing, we would wake up and someone would say, "What happened?"

While we were conducting shore bombardment during daylight, the carrier planes were conducting bombing attacks and they were subjected to AA fire from the Japs. On several occasions the *Aylwin* would leave the formation to pick up pilots from planes that were damaged and had landed in the water. One afternoon when the carrier planes were returning from a raid, one of our new destroyers, which had not seen much action, mistook these planes as Japanese and took them under fire.

The lead F6F was shot down and we went over, at high speed, to see if the pilot had survived. It turned out that he was very much alive and he was the air group commander from that carrier. He was so mad I thought he would explode. He loved that plane and now it was gone.

During the latter part of June, the *Aylwin* was released from the Task Force, and proceeded back to Eniwetok Island for upkeep and repairs. We were anchored in the lagoon and again got liberty ashore. This time we were allowed to swim off the ship. We also had a long awaited delivery of mail from home. One of the mail deliveries brought a letter from Virginia telling me that our son James had been born on July 2nd, and that she and the baby were doing just fine. I really felt proud to be a father and was anxious to get home and see the little fellow.

About the middle of July we joined another group of ships and proceeded back to Guam. During the trip to Guam, several gunnery and radar tracking exercises were conducted. The latter was conducted at night, with one ship steaming away from the formation and getting outside of radar detection range. This target ship then started closing in on the formation.

When we arrived at Guam, we again took up shore bombardment duties near Asan beach. This was done to protect the Underwater Demolition Team (UDT) working near the beach to clear a path for boats to make a landing. After several days we moved to an area near Agana Bay. A different activity occurred one day when we were ordered to destroy a Japanese mine which had broken from its mooring and was floating on the surface. We steamed over to the mine and took it under fire with 40mm guns and nothing happened. So we opened up with one of our 5-inch guns and got the mine to explode.

One afternoon while furnishing fire support to the marines, I was talking to the Chief Fire Controlman up in the gun director when he saw a Japanese ship coming out of Agana Bay. He asked me, "Shall we take it under fire?" Of course I said yes and so we started shelling it with our 5-inch guns. After a few direct hits it started to sink and finally sank right in the harbor entrance. The *Aylwin* caught hell for that, as it blocked the harbor entrance and tugs had to be called in to haul away the wreckage.

On 30 July, our duty with the Task Force was completed and we passed almost all of our 5-inch ammunition to our sister ship, the *Colahan*, and took station to escort the *New Mexico* back to Eniwetok Atoll. After refueling at Eniwetok the following ships, *New Mexico*, cruisers *San Francisco & St. Louis* and the destroyers *Dale*, *Farragut & Aylwin* got underway for Pearl Harbor. The trip back to Pearl Harbor was just like being on a vacation cruise. We did have to stand radio watches, but we did not have to conduct gunnery exercises since we had no more ammunition since leaving the forward area. We were all happy at the thought of going back to the States and everyone was joking and smiling, knowing that we would soon be back home.

After arriving at Pearl Harbor and refueling, the *New Mexico* and the same destroyers left Pearl Harbor enroute to Puget Sound Navy Yard for extensive overhaul.

14

Return to States
&
Commissioning

The trip from Pearl Harbor to the Puget Sound Navy Yard in the state of Washington was uneventful but everyone was really happy to be going back to the states once again.

As we were steaming through Juan de Fuca strait leading to Seattle and the Bremerton Navy yard, we were cold as we had come from a warm climate and it was a cloudy and windy day there in the state of Washington.

We had gone below to our lockers and gotten our pea coats and were standing on deck looking at the houses on shore. Suddenly, one of the fellows said, "Look at that." We all turned to get a good look and we could see some kids swimming in the water. We got so cold just looking at them that we all went inside to get warmed up again. It sure was good looking at the U.S. again, and seeing all of the houses and buildings in Seattle gave us a real good feeling. We had been away for a long time, seen a lot of action and here we were without a scratch, back in the states. We all had a lot to be thankful for coming back in such good condition.

We arrived at Puget Sound Navy Yards on August 17th, and after we were tied up in the navy yard we received several sacks of mail. We were having a good time catching up on our loved ones' events while we were gone. Before finishing reading all of my mail, I got word to report to the captain in the officer's wardroom. I arrived at the same time as our chief fire controlman, Worrell, and when we entered the wardroom the captain stood up, shook our hands and said, "Congratulations, you are both now commissioned officers with the rank of ensign."

This meant that we were now *Mustangs*. Mustang is the term for any Navy commissioned officer who came up through the enlisted ranks. He explained that once we obtained our new uniforms, we would have to be transferred off the *Aylwin*, as the Navy Regulations stated that we could no longer serve on the ship where we had been blue jackets.

This made both of us very sad as we had so many friends on board and we knew all of the equipment on board and how to keep it running at peak performance.

I went ashore and, after ordering my uniforms, I called Virginia and we had a great time talking. We both wanted to get together, so I asked her to pack up and bring our son James up to Puget Sound. Then, we could wait out my next assignment together. I had been told that it would probably be about a month before I would hear from Washington.

A week later I met Virginia in Seattle where she had come up from San Francisco by train. It sure was great seeing her again and James sure did look good. He was a robust and healthy looking little boy. We had to take a ferryboat from Seattle to the Navy Yard and, as we were sitting waiting for the ferry, I was holding Jim on my lap. All of a sudden, I felt something very warm on my leg and when I held him up his diaper had leaked and the leg of my uniform pants was really wet.

When we got to the Navy base I checked in and we got an apartment in Port Orchard. We proceeded to our new home, unpacked and went to the store to stock up the kitchen. Port Orchard was quite a distance from the Navy base and I first had to take a bus and then a boat to get to the Yard. After a few days, they told me just to call and not to bother to come to the base to see if they had received my orders. That gave Virginia and me some needed time together and we sure did enjoy that time.

We even got a babysitter a couple of evenings and went to Seattle for dinner at a hotel. On another occasion we got to see a show.

After about four weeks, my orders arrived and I had to report to the Officers School in Boston. We packed up everything, got our tickets for the train trip and headed to Seattle to catch our train.

This was quite a trip going completely across country with a new baby. We were not able to get a single train all of the way across, so we had many stops and transfers to other trains. On one of the trains had wicker seats in old coaches, which must have been built in the 1800s. The heat was from an old pot-belly stove in the middle of the coach. In order to take care of the baby, either Virginia or I would have to go to a more modern coach to find a wash room to bathe and change him. When it was time for Jim to eat, we would get a bottle of milk heated and I would cross my legs and prop him up and he would start to drink. He would drain the bottle so fast that the other servicemen would gather around and watch.

At first it was hard to get him asleep, so I would take him out to the part of the coach where it was coupled to the next car. The sound of the wheels going clickety-clack on the rails would put him right to sleep. Sleep for us was another matter as the seats did not make for a very good bed. So by the time we reached Chicago, we were both pretty well beat. From Chicago on to Boston we had a more modern coach and we were able to get better rest.

Even though the train was uncomfortable, it sure was enjoyable to see the good old USA as we went along. There were times in the Pacific when I wondered if I would ever get another chance to see the states again, so it sure looked good to sit and stare out the window as we rolled along. Even some of the run down sections of towns we went by looked good as this was our great USA.

If I were taking that trip today, I would probably get bored just sitting and looking at the scenery go by. But at that time I was so thankful to have gotten back alive and in one piece, that these sights totally consumed my interests.

15

Officers' Schools
&
New Construction

After the long trip across country by train, we arrived in Boston where I was to attend an officer's radar class at Harvard. I checked in at the school and obtained a listing of rooms to rent in town while we were in Boston. We finally decided on a nice home on Beacon Street.

It was an old house with three floors. It had a large entrance hall with a big chandelier hanging from the top of the third floor. There was also a grand piano in this entrance hall. It was quite an impressive home and we were quite comfortable in our rooms.

The lady of the house took quite a liking to Jim and she would put him next to her on the piano bench and play tunes for him. He really liked it and she had a good time with him. It sure was a welcome time for us, as it gave us a chance to spend time together alone. The lady of the house also babysat for us so that we could get out at night for dinner and a show. It was a great time. We were living in a real nice house with a built-in babysitter and good meals. I hadn't had it so good for three years.

The first school I attended was one to train electronic officers in the upkeep and repair of typical air search radar. There were three of us in the class who had been radar technicians and we already knew the equipment. One day the instructor replaced a good tube in one of the indicator units with a bad one. He called us in and said we would have an hour to find the failure. While he waited, he was going to go and get a cup of coffee. The three of us knew right away what the trouble was. Since there were several identical units in the room, we went over to one that was not in use and borrowed a good tube, replaced the bad one. We turned the equipment on and it operated just fine.

We then sat around and swapped sea stories until the instructor returned. We told him there was nothing wrong with the equipment, as he could see it was running normally. He shut it down and pulled the tube out where he had installed one with a pin cut off. As soon as he saw a good tube, he smiled and wanted to know where his bad tube was.

After completing the air search school, we were transferred over to a class on fire control radar at Massachusettes Institute of Technology. This was a much more interesting experience as we got to look at some of the new equipment being developed for the fleet. The engineers working on this new equipment also showed us a first model of an electronic computer. All of the active components in the system were vacuum tubes and there were over a hundred various tubes.

They told us that the whole system could not be run reliably, because they couldn't seem to get all of the tubes to work at the same time. Every time they tried to make a run, the system would crash after a short time and they would find several tubes burned out. Of course, transistors had not been developed at that time.

Our time in Boston was a real vacation, in that it gave Virginia and me a chance to get to know each other better and we got to know Jim. It also gave us a chance to get out and see some of the sights in the Boston area:

- The Charles River
- Cambridge
- Old South Meeting Hall
- King's Chapel
- Old North Church
- The Beacon Hill area.

After completing the two schools in the Boston area, I received orders to report to the officers receiving area in Norfolk, Virginia. So we bid good-bye to the nice landlady we had in Boston, packed and caught the train to Norfolk.

When we arrived at the Navy yard, I checked in and we were assigned quarters in a hotel across the harbor. We loaded our luggage, caught a boat and checked in that afternoon. It was a pleasant location and the room was really nice. It had a wonderful view from the window. There was a bedroom and a living room, which was good, because we could put Jim to bed in one room, close the door, and we could talk and listen to the radio without disturbing him.

Each morning I had to ride the boat over to the Navy Yard and attend classes. That part was pretty dull, since I had already been to sea and these classes were telling new officers about life at sea.

One night we were sitting talking and Jim started to cry. I told Virginia he was getting spoiled and to just let him cry it out. When he didn't stop after a while, we finally went in to see what was the matter.

He had rolled off the surface of the bed and was wedged between the bed and the steam heating unit. We had to pack him up and take him to the nearest hospital to get the burns treated and bandaged up.

After about a month in Norfolk, I received orders to proceed to Orange, Texas, to be part of the crew on a new destroyer that was being built there. We packed up again and traveled by train, and bus, to Orange where we were assigned quarters in an apartment building. This place was really crummy and dirty, but we settled in and made the best of it.

We were able to meet the other officers and their wives while we did the last bit of outfitting the new ship. This ship was the *U.S.S. HAWKINS DD873*, a large Summer class destroyer that had been designed after WWII started.

On the *Aylwin*, we had four 5-inch guns and the *Hawkins* has six with two guns in each of three turrets. The *Hawkins* also had more 40mm guns and newer radar, radio and sonar equipment.

Of course the newest thing for me was to live in officer's country. I was assigned to a stateroom that I shared with the communications officer, LT Robert Manley. Like the other officers on board, he was a nice fellow and we got along just fine.

This was quite a change from living on board the *Aylwin*, because we now had thick mattress, plenty of hanging space for uniforms, desks with drawers and a small safe for each of us.

All of our officers were well qualified. Our skipper, Commander Iverson, had been in command of a destroyer during the Guadalcanal campaign and had been awarded the Navy Cross for action up the slot.

Our Exec, LT Peter Coy, had also been on destroyers in the Guadalcanal operations, as had several others.

We had a great engineering officer, LT Ed Letscher, and our gunner officer was LT Conrad Meyer III. All had extensive experience during the first three years of our involvement in WWII. We had a total of 18 officers assigned, whereas the *Aylwin* had only about 10 when I left.

USS Hawkins DD873

16

Plank Owner
&
Back to Sea

Plank owner is the Navy term for a member of the crew of a new ship when it is placed in commission as a U.S. Navy vessel. Since I was one of the officers assigned to the *Hawkins* when it was commissioned, I became a plank owner. The *Hawkins* was sure a change from the *Aylwin*.

It was bigger, had more guns and the latest radar and sonar equipment. My assignment was as the electronics officer in charge of all of the radar, sonar and radio equipment on board. I would also be standing watches in the combat information center (CIC) and on the coding board.

After the ship was put in commission, I packed up Virginia and Jim and took them to the Naval Air Station. There they caught a C-47 bound for Alameda Naval Air Station. We got underway the next morning and proceeded to the Underway Training Unit at Guantanamo Bay, Cuba for shakedown training. Shakedown training is conducted under way at sea by the training unit, who observe and grade the crew's performance during the tests.

After completing the underway training the *Hawkins* received orders to proceed to the Norfolk Navy Yard for conversion to a radar picket ship. This involved removal of some guns in the aft part of the ship, installation of a new tripod mast aft for support, and a new high-powered air search and height finding radar. The conversion also involved adding more very high frequency (VHF) radio equipment for communication with our fighter planes and adding equipment in the CIC room. With the addition of the high powered microwave air search radar the ship would have been top heavy, so they removed our torpedo tubes.

By this time we had been receiving word about how many radar picket ships were being destroyed by Japanese kamikaze planes around Okinawa, and the idea of being outfitted to become sitting ducks for this type of attack did not sit too well with us.

I was a little scared, but as the ship conducted antiaircraft firing exercises I began to feel more confident that we would make out all right. We had the best air search radar equipment. We had excellent air control officers, our radar operators and CIC personnel were all well qualified. Our gunnery officer was very well-experienced. The fire control radar and computer equipment was the best, and our gun crews were shaping up to be very excellent gunners.

After another underway training session at Guantanamo Bay, we headed for the Panama Canal, and then up to San Diego, where we conducted air control exercises with F6F fighters from the Naval Air Station at San Diego. These were getting to be more exciting times working with aircraft and communicating with them on a daily basis. We had two officers on board who were qualified air controllers and it was really interesting watching them work with the fighter planes of the combat air patrol (CAP). We had an enlarged CIC to handle the extra radar equipment and radio equipment, and it was beginning to gave us a real feeling of confidence that we could handle the Kamikaze attacks. We should be able to vector our CAP fighters to shoot down the enemy planes and, if any did get through, we had real good gun crews to take them down. The closer a Kamikaze comes, the more accurate the gunfire becomes, and with the number of antiaircraft guns we most probably could score a direct hit before the plane can crash on the ship.

After a short stay in San Diego we got underway for Pearl Harbor with a carrier and several other destroyers and cruisers. We all stopped at Pearl Harbor to refuel and take on stores and ammunition. We didn't stay long at Pearl and were soon underway for the Western Pacific to join the Carrier Task Force. En route, we continued various exercises, and of course, the sunrise and sunset General Quarters.

As we passed Truk Atoll the carrier planes raided the Japanese positions there but we did not experience any return air attacks. Apparently, most of their aircraft had been destroyed by previous carrier attacks. Truk was bypassed in the march toward Japan and no landings were ever made on it by our forces up to that time.

We were still several days from joining up with our Task Force when we received word of an atomic bomb that had been dropped on Hiroshima. Another was dropped on Nagasaki just two days later, and before we joined the Task Force the war was declared over.

Everybody on board the *Hawkins* was overjoyed to get the news. Most of us had been at sea for more than two years, and we had more than enough of wondering if our number was up.

We heard about some sort of an atomic bomb and how powerful it was, but we had no idea what they were talking about.

Even though the hostilities had been declared at an end, we continued our westward journey to join up with Task Force 58.

17

The End of World War II

PEACE AT LAST

We finally arrived to find the Task Force already at anchor in Tokyo Bay. It was a beautiful sight seeing all of our ships and the surrounding land. We saw Mt. Fujiyama in the background and it made a beautiful view.

After a day or so, we were ordered to go to the Yokosuka Naval base and tie up to a pier there. This gave us a chance to get ashore and see some of the sights. The first places that I got to see ashore were some of the shops in the navy yard. The Japanese had dug long tunnels in the hillside and then made rooms along the tunnels for various repair shops. In one of these shops I found a repair facility for their search radar systems. I was amazed at how crude their air search radar was compared to the ones we had. The system that we had before 1941, which was an experimental system, was much better than this equipment. I was unable to find any microwave radar system for surface search and no fire control system.

I finally got liberty to go ashore into Tokyo and see some of the sights. The train ride from Yokosuka to Tokyo was quite an experience. All of the passenger cars had their seats removed to make more room for passengers. There were so many people in the boarding area that we had to keep from being pushed around. As the train pulled in, I could see that each car was packed with people standing up. As it came to a stop, I saw a woman on the train hold a baby out the window so that he could urinate. When the doors opened to the cars, there were several policemen at each door. After the departing passengers had left, they formed a line with their nightsticks and started pushing boarding passengers through the door. They were packed in each car like sardines.

We did not feel like getting trapped in that mess, so we stood on the outside step of the car holding on to a handrail all the way to Tokyo. Sounds a little dangerous, but we were young and anxious to get to town.

When we first got to town we made our way out of the business area to look at the residential area. When we finally got to the residential area, the devastation was so great that it was an awesome picture. The living areas were mostly made of bamboo and the firebomb raids by our B-52s had sure done their work. Block after block was just a pile of rubble in the middle of the each block. Destruction in these areas was complete and I don't have any idea where the displaced people were living, but they must have been commuting from outside of Tokyo.

We were surprised at the crude cars and trucks we saw. Most of these vehicles were run by charcoal burners, which were mounted on small trailers behind the vehicle. At this stage of things the Japanese relied mostly on electric trains and streetcars for transportation. The streetcars were in good shape and were still running well. It was interesting patrolling the downtown streets of Tokyo and seeing how they lived. At about noontime, we passed construction workers eating lunch and most seemed to be eating a ball of rice about the size of a tennis ball.

We had quite a time seeing the sights in the downtown area, finding statues of Buddha, among others, and seeing some of their temples. There were large ponds around with very large gold fish. I had never seen anything like it up to that time. We made the trip back to Yokosuka the same way we had made it to Tokyo, riding on the step outside of the car. It got to be fun after a while. At least we had fresh air and we weren't crowded.

A few days later, one of the Radio Technicians came to me and said that he had an uncle that had been interned during the war in a resort up in the mountain area.

He wanted to look him up, but he needed an officer to escort him to the site. I agreed to go with him and we took off for the train station. We didn't know which train to take, so we got a schedule. Unfortunately, it was in Japanese, and we couldn't identify any trains. We finally found a conductor and we held the schedule up, to point to the city we were headed to. He motioned for us to follow him and he took us to the right platform, pointed to the train number and showed us on his watch what time it would arrive.

There were quite a few Japanese waiting with us, and as we looked over the crowd, we noticed most of them just came up to our shoulders. Then, down toward the end of the platform, we spotted a Japanese fellow who was almost as tall as we. We worked our way down to his position and found that he spoke English. It turned out that he was a Japanese-American from Los Angeles. He had been in Tokyo in December of 1941 on business and was interned for the duration.

We made good connections after the train arrived and this train was not as crowded as the one to Tokyo, so we stood inside. When we arrived at the station at the foot of the mountain, we found we then had to take a cog car up the mountain.

This car ran on a zigzag track up the mountain. It would start, climb up an incline and then stop. The driver would then take the controls, go to the other end of the car and switch to the next incline going the opposite direction. He would then repeat this process all of the way to the top. After arriving, we walked to the resort hotel where the technician found his uncle and we had a nice lunch and tea. Even though his uncle was American, he had been in business in Japan for a number of years and was treated very well during the war years.

This was a most interesting trip and the scenery was beautiful going both ways. It was an experience that not many U.S. servicemen have had a chance to enjoy.

Since the war was now over, many of us who had served since 1941 started to wonder when we would be getting off of the ship and going home.

Finally, the message from the Bureau of Personnel arrived outlining the requirements for release from active duty. I was one of six officers qualified to be transported back to the U.S. and released from active duty. We could hardly wait to get going.

Short Timers of the Hawkins

The picture above shows the six of us just after we got the word to pack up and get ready to be transferred. From left to right, Henry Trist, assistant Gunnery Officer; Ervin Baumrucker, CIC and Fighter Director Officer; Conrad Meyer III, Gunnery Officer; Peter Coy, Executive Officer; your writer; and Dick Winter, First Lieutenant.

We were transferred to the commander Service Forces and assigned to various troop transports for the trip back to the states. I did not get the chance to ride back with any of the other five, but I soon made friends with the other junior officers on the trip back. We were assigned to one of the regular troop quarters with bunks stacked three high, but they had installed some canvas tarps to separate us from the enlisted passengers. We also had a separate eating area and, when meals were finished, the table was soon being used for a poker game. It went on for the two whole week trip back to San Diego. I was amazed at the amount of money that changed hands every day. There was no entertainment on board, no books, papers or movies, so those of us in the sleeping area where I was did play blackjack every day, but not for money, just for match sticks.

The transport did not stop in San Francisco, but went on down the coast to San Diego. There, we disembarked and reported into the Receiving Station. The first thing I did was to find a phone to call Virginia to let her know I was back. As soon as I could, I boarded a bus for San Francisco and headed home. Upon arriving in San Francisco, I was given a glorious welcome by Virginia and our new son Jim. Jim didn't remember me at first, but soon took to me. It sure was good to be back home in one piece and now the only thing left to do was to get released from active duty.

The next morning, I reported into the Separation Center on Treasure Island. By the end of that week I was a civilian again.

Virginia had an apartment in San Francisco and of course I packed all of my things in her apartment and settled right in. One of the first things was to get some civilian clothes. I contacted my mother in Topeka and requested that she ship my clothes to San Francisco. Mother informed me that she and my dad had figured that I most probably would not survive, so they had given all of my things away. One of the big jobs was to get new clothes.

At the Separation Center on Treasure Island, I was told how much it would be worth in the long run to stay in the Naval Reserve. I would probably have to go on two weeks active duty each year, and attend drills each month, but there would be pay for this. So I signed up to stay in the Reserves.

This brings a close to my narrative of the experiences I had during World War II.

EPILOGUE

I started my active duty in May 1941 when I was 19 years old and when separated from active duty in September 1945 I was 23 years of age. I entered as an apprentice seaman and was an Ensign when reporting in for separation. I soon found out that my commission as Ensign was only temporary and before separation I was reduced back to First Class Radio Technician. As an enlisted man the Navy would only transport me back to my point of enlistment in Topeka, Kansas. They would not ship my family back. Therefore we decided to stay in Virginia's apartment and I would see about getting back to school at University of California at Berkeley to pick up where I left off at KU in 1941.

I met many fine people while serving on the two destroyers and I was blessed in not having been wounded in any of the actions. I will always remember the experiences that I had, the good and the bad ones. It is significant that my memories of the good times are much stronger than that of the not so good. I feel that I was extremely lucky to have been able to be in so many significant operations and to have seen so much action.

Prior to being called up for active duty in the Navy the extent of my travels outside of Topeka, Kansas was a trip to Chicago, when I was 10 or 12 years old and a trip to Colorado Springs when I was about 12 or 13 years old. I feel that I had aged more in the 4 ½ year period of active duty than at any other times. I knew that it was time for me to be on my own and to be ready to take care of my new family.

In one of the briefings that we had at Treasure Island before being separated, a financial expert described the advantages of staying in the Naval Reserve. He pointed out that we could take two weeks of training each year with pay and, after reaching age 60, we could expect a good retirement pay based on our active duty time and reserve time. I did stay in the reserve and after a month or two I received my permanent commission as an Ensign dated back to my temporary appointment. It was a good choice even though I was recalled to active duty during the Korean Conflict for two more years. That time of active duty was again very interesting and beneficial in that it resulted in advancement to full Lieutenant. At the end of my reserve service, my rank was full Commander.

Not bad for an old mustang.

REFERENCES

Costello, John. *The Pacific War: 1941-1945*. New York City: Quill, 1981.

Layton, Edwin. *And I Was There*. New York: Wm. Morrow & Co., Inc., 1985.

Prados, John. *Combined Fleet Decoded*. Annapolis: Naval Institute Press, 1995.

Prange, Gordon. *Miracle at Midway*. New York: McGraw-Hill Book Co., 1982.

USS Aylwin Deck Logs, 1942-1944. Washington, D.C.: U.S. Navy Archives, 1944.

USS Aylwin DD355 History. Washington, D.C.: U.S. Navy Archives, 1944.

Van DerVatt, Dan. *The Pacific Campaign*. New York: Simon & Schuster, 1991.

Willmott, H.P. *The Barrier & the Javelin*, Annapolis: Naval Institute Press, 1983.

GLOSSARY OF TERMS

ASW
Anti-Submarine Warfare

AFT
Anything behind midship

AFTER CON
Station where ship can be controlled if bridge is damaged

BANDIT
Radar contact identified as enemy

BELOW
Areas below main deck

BOGIE
Unidentified radar contact

CAP
Combat Air Patrol

CIC
Combat Information Center

CINCPAC
Commander in Chief Pacific Fleet

BOW
Point at the front of the ship

CON
Controlling the sailing of the ship

DRT
Dead Reckoning Tracer

FANTAIL
Main deck area at the rear of the ship

FATHOMETER
Sound system for measuring depth of water

FIGHTER DIRECTOR OFFICER (FDO)
Directs fighter aircraft to target using radar information

FOE'C'SLE
Deck just behind the bow

FORWARD
Anything in front of midship

GENERAL QUARTERS (GQ)
Battle stations

GYROCOMPASS
Compass using a gyro

HALYARDS
Vertical rope lines

HEAD
Bathroom and Toilet

IFF
Identification Friend or Foe

LADDER
Stairs between decks

LSO
Landing Signal Officer

MAIN BATTERY
Five inch guns

MESS HALL
Dining area

MIDSHIP
relating to or located at the middle of the ship

MUSTANG
An enlisted man who has been commissioned as an officer

OFFICER-OF-THE-DECK (OOD)
Officer in charge when Captain is not on deck

PORT
The left side or anything to the left

RADAR
Radio Detection And Ranging

ROTC
Reserve Officer Training Corp

SECURE
Cease current activity

SONAR
Sound Detection And Ranging

SORTIE
One mission or attack

STARBOARD
The right side or anything to the right

STERN
The rear of the ship

TF
Task Force

TINCANS
Destroyers

TOPSIDE
Any area on main deck or above in the open

VECTOR 110
Come to course 110

YARDARM
Horizontal arms near the top of the main mast

U.S. NAVY AIRCRAFT:

AVENGER   TBF, torpedo and bomber
CATALINA   PBY, Twin engine scout seaplane
CORSAIR   F4U, Fighter
DAUNTLESS   SBD, scout and dive bombers
DEVASTATOR   TBD, Torpedo
HELLCAT   F6F, Fighters
WILDCAT   F4F, Fighters

JAPANESE NAVY AIRCRAFT:

BETTY   Land based twin engine bombers
CLAUD   Fighters
KATE   Torpedo bombers
MAVIS   Scout seaplanes
NELL   Dive bombers
VAL   Dive bombers
ZEKE or ZERO   Fighters

Printed in the United States
19353LVS00001B/506